"I want to prove that ghosts exist, and you guys had an opening in my area of expertise just as I graduated. Kind of seems like fate."

"What's your area?" Blaine liked Flynn's attitude already, though. He wasn't going into it predisposed to disbelief. He wanted to prove ghosts existed, like Blaine.

"Electromagnetism, biology, and computers. I've written a few programs to crunch the data for temperature changes, etc. And they can totally be tweaked as needed. Plus… well, I guess you guys are the ones for whom this is a pro not a con, but I've experienced ghosts before."

"Yeah? When?" That wasn't particularly unique. Ghosts were everywhere, and people also got spooked by things that *weren't* ghosts all the time.

"Most of my life, actually." Flynn held his gaze for a long moment, and Blaine felt like the guy was testing him. He must have passed because Flynn continued. "My parents died when I was five. Car accident. Every now and then, when I really need her, my mother comes to me."

WELCOME TO

DREAMSPUN BEYOND

Dear Reader,

Love is the dream. It dazzles us, makes us stronger, and brings us to our knees. Dreamspun Desires tell stories of love featuring your favorite heartwarming heroes, captivating plots, and exotic locations. Stories that make your breath catch and your imagination soar.

In the pages of these wonderful love stories, readers can escape to a world where love conquers all, the tenderness of a first kiss sweeps you away, and your heart pounds at the sight of the one you love.

When you put it all together, you find romance in its truest form.

Love always finds a way.

Elizabeth North

Executive Director
Dreamspinner Press

Sean Michael

THE SUPERS

PUBLISHED BY

Published by
DREAMSPINNER PRESS

5032 Capital Circle SW, Suite 2, PMB# 279,
Tallahassee, FL 32305-7886 USA
www.dreamspinnerpress.com

This is a work of fiction. Names, characters, places, and incidents either
are the product of author imagination or are used fictitiously, and any
resemblance to actual persons, living or dead, business establishments,
events, or locales is entirely coincidental.

The Supers
© 2017 Sean Michael.

Cover Art
© 2017 Aaron Anderson.
aaronbydesign55@gmail.com
Cover content is for illustrative purposes only and any person depicted
on the cover is a model.

ISBN: 978-1-63533-889-8
Digital ISBN: 978-1-63533-890-4
Library of Congress Control Number: 2017905517
Published October 2017
v. 1.0

Printed in the United States of America

∞

This paper meets the requirements of
ANSI/NISO Z39.48-1992 (Permanence of Paper).

Often referred to as "Space Cowboy" and "Gangsta of Love" while still striving for the moniker of "Maurice," **SEAN MICHAEL** spends his days surfing, smutting, organizing his immense gourd collection and fantasizing about one day retiring on a small secluded island peopled entirely by horseshoe crabs. While collecting vast amounts of vintage gay pulp novels and mood rings, Sean whiles away the hours between dropping the f-bomb and pursuing the Kama Sutra by channeling the long-lost spirit of John Wayne and singing along with the soundtrack to Chicago.

A longtime writer of complicated haiku, currently Sean is attempting to learn the advanced arts of plate spinning and soap carving sex toys.

Barring any of that? He'll stick with writing his stories, thanks, and rubbing pretty bodies together to see if they spark.

Website: www.seanmichaelwrites.com

Blog: seanmichaelwrites.blogspot.ca

Facebook: www.facebook.com/
SeanMichaelWrites

Twitter: @seanmichael09

By Sean Michael

DREAMSPUN BEYOND
#6 – The Supers

DREAMSPUN DESIRES
#39 – The Teddy Bear Club

Published by **DREAMSPINNER PRESS**
www.dreamspinnerpress.com

Chapter One

"OKAY, Mrs. Michaels. I have two pounds of tomatoes, a bunch of spinach, and some okra. You want anything else?" The heat was hanging on today, the sun beating down on the makeshift building that was the official King and Franks Farm Stand, named after his mom and dad's families.

"No, Blaine, honey. That's it. How's your mom?"

"Good. Good. The chemo is done, and she's recovering. She's a stud." And Dad was Dad—working his ass off on the organic farm that kept them in quarters. One day Blaine would go back to college, get a job that helped out, but for now they needed him here, working the stand, hawking veggies.

It was a good life, really. He hated being cooped up, hated being trapped under fluorescent lights, and the idea of a cubicle made him gag.

And this way he got to work with the Supers on the side. Well, at night really, as that's when they tended to do their thing. They hadn't had a gig in a few weeks, but then they hadn't had anyone doing tech work since Jill left. She'd moved from Port Hope to BC with her girlfriend.

Jason had found someone new, though, had promised to bring him by today to meet Blaine.

His folks teased him about being a spirit chaser, but they indulged him. Hell, he was a grown-up; they didn't have the right to tell him no, but still....

The guys were important to him. They believed him—mostly.

He hoped the new guy wasn't too much of a skeptic. It was hard to find tech guys who believed that ghosts might be real. They'd discovered when they'd first banded together that most tech guys were there to prove that ghosts *didn't* exist.

The huge van pulled up, Supernatural Explorers written on the side of it. The thing fit all their equipment, six people—though there were usually just four—and in a pinch a couple of them could sleep in there too.

Jason, who ran the group and got them gigs and stuff; Darnell, their cameraman; and Will, their, well, roadie for want of a better word, all spilled out, with another guy in tow. He had to be the new guy, and he was handsome. He didn't look much like a scientist. More like a football player. Tall, broad-chested, with dark curls that spilled around his face in an unruly manner, the guy was quite handsome.

Blaine knew what *he* looked like—a dishwater-blond hippie with dirt under his fingernails and torn-up clothes. He was a child of the earth, after all.

Jason was skinny as a rail, had an acne-ridden face, and wore glasses. Darnell was a stud, milk-chocolate skin accompanied by the most amazing dreads, while Will looked like a biker and had the muscles to move any equipment they brought with them. They were a scruffy crew who didn't quite look like they belonged together, but they were ghost hunters—they weren't exactly hired for their matching attire, and not a one of them was interested in wearing a uniform.

Jason gave Blaine a wide grin and waved at the new guy. "This is Flynn Huntington, potential com tech. Flynn, this is Blaine, the guy who has the final say on whether or not you've got the job."

Flynn held out his hand and gave him a friendly smile. "Nice to meet you. So you're the leader of this motley crew?"

"Me?" He'd never led the guys anywhere but into trouble. "I'm not the leader. I'm just the flashlight guy."

Blaine was the one who tended to see something if there was something to see. He heard them—the ghosts—talking to him, but it wasn't clear. It was like a constant, crazy murmuring.

"Like I said, he who leads." Flynn winked, and when he reached out and shook Blaine's hand, a flash of something sparked between them. Flynn must have felt it too. His eyes widened, his mouth opening on a soft gasp.

A rush of heat and pleasure and a jolt of something dangerous, and this had never happened to Blaine, ever, so it couldn't be real. Had to be the heat.

It wasn't until Flynn dropped his hand that Blaine realized he'd still been holding it. Flynn's smile seemed warmer this time.

"We all grilled him and gave him the okay, but now it's your turn," Jason informed him, looking around.

"I'll man the stand if you want to take him to the side or something. I don't mean to press you, but we've got a gig this weekend."

"Just watch the cash, okay?"

Jason gave him a hurt look. "Dude, how many summers did I work here?"

"Yeah, yeah. You're right." This was the first summer, though, where it felt a little like life and death. They needed every penny they could scrape together to pay the fucking hospital bills.

Flynn followed Blaine to a quiet corner, and Blaine was overly conscious that as tall as he was, Flynn was taller. Seriously, he hadn't known they built scientists in extrastudly.

"So, why us? Why this? Tell me everything." He grabbed a plum from a basket and tossed it over.

Flynn grabbed it easily and rubbed it against his shirt. "Thanks." He took a bite, the juice running down from one corner of his mouth.

Blaine was struck with the urge to lick it away. He forced himself to look into Flynn's eyes instead.

"I want to prove that ghosts exist, and you guys had an opening in my area of expertise just as I graduated. Kind of seems like fate."

"What's your area?" Blaine liked Flynn's attitude already, though. He wasn't going into it predisposed to disbelief. He wanted to prove ghosts existed, like Blaine.

"Electromagnetism, biology, and computers. I've written a few programs to crunch the data for temperature changes, etc. And they can totally be tweaked as needed. Plus… well, I guess you guys are the ones for whom this is a pro not a con, but I've experienced ghosts before."

"Yeah? When?" That wasn't particularly unique. Ghosts were everywhere, and people also got spooked by things that *weren't* ghosts all the time.

"Most of my life, actually." Flynn held his gaze for a long moment, and Blaine felt like the guy was testing him. He must have passed because Flynn continued. "My parents died when I was five. Car accident. Every now and then, when I really need her, my mother comes to me."

"I'm sorry, man. Honestly." Blaine knew the fear of losing his folks. He lived in terror of losing his mom, especially now.

Flynn shook his head. "It was a long time ago, and like I said, I still have my mother when I really need her." This time his grin was self-deprecating. "Of course I learned early not to tell people about it. I've experienced other phenomena too, that I know were from beyond, so I want to prove it."

Prove I'm not crazy.

Though unsaid, Blaine was pretty sure he could hear that in Flynn's thoughts.

"I get that. I don't need proof. I know like I know chairs exist, but I'm the guy in the group the spirits seem to flock to."

"That's got to be scary sometimes. I mean when it's a place where people were murdered. Or a prison or something."

"Sometimes. Lots of times. Mostly it turns out to be nothing—creaking buildings or animals—but sometimes...." At least Blaine thought so. He was pretty sure.

"Yeah, I imagine there's a lot of dead ends." Flynn stopped for a moment. Then he laughed, the deep sound finding a place to settle in Blaine's belly. "Pun not intended, but damn, it should have been."

Blaine began to laugh along, and suddenly Darnell appeared. "So, he's in, huh? Cool."

"That quick?" Flynn asked.

Darnell nodded, his dreads flopping enthusiastically. "Dude, you made him laugh out loud. That's a thing."

"I didn't even do it on purpose!" Flynn looked pleased, dark eyes lit up and twinkling.

"We'll give it a try. I think we'll manage," Blaine said. And if they didn't, who cared?

"That's great!" Flynn grabbed Blaine's hand and shook it, and again there was a jolt, a sharing almost of… spirit?

Lord, he was getting crazier as the day went on.

Flynn finished the plum as Darnell called the others over. They all shook hands, and nobody else seemed to feel anything special when they touched Flynn.

Huh. Well, maybe Blaine was imagining things. It happened. A guy could start reading into everything.

"We should go out to celebrate," Darnell suggested. "Have supper, a couple of beers, and get to know each other before we go to work this weekend."

"Sure. I'm free," Flynn noted.

"I am too, unless something comes up with Mom," Blaine agreed.

"Your mom?" Flynn asked.

"She's battling breast cancer."

Flynn winced. "I'm sorry, man. That sucks." Flynn slid his hand over Blaine's, squeezed.

"Thank you. She's going to make it. I have faith." And Dad needed her.

"That's half the battle, isn't it?" Flynn gave him a sympathetic smile.

"You ready to go now, or do we need to meet you at Bennie's?" Darnell asked him.

"I have to close out, go home and change, shower. All that shit."

"So we'll meet you there. Promise I won't let Jase and Will get too shit-faced before you show up." Darnell winked and popped Flynn in the arm. "Let's go, man. First drink is on the newbie."

Flynn chuckled. "How come I feel like I'm being shaken down?"

"If they offer to buy you a cement mixer, say no!" Blaine called.

Flynn frowned, and the last thing Blaine heard was Flynn asking, "What's a cement mixer?" followed by Darnell's cackling laugh.

Oh man. He was going to have to hurry, or they were going to eat Mr. Flynn Huntington alive. He started closing out, trying not to get distracted by the memory of Flynn's dancing eyes.

Chapter Two

FLYNN had refused the offer of a "cement mixer," silently thanking the still-absent Blaine for the heads-up. He had bought the guys two rounds already but barely started on his own second beer. He hadn't eaten all day, aside from a plum, so his tolerance was lower than usual. Once Blaine got here, they were going to eat, and then he could indulge.

He didn't want to be shit-faced tonight, not with his new… coworkers? Team? Let him prove himself capable first, then he could let it all hang out.

The guys were a hoot, honestly, and seemed to be decent, genuinely interested, and basically all-around good guys. They were clearly friends, which was nice. For the kind of work they did, it was important everyone got along, cared.

Things could—at least so he hoped—get odd and intense in their investigations. He wanted powerful and magical and strange. He wanted to prove that ghosts were real. That death wasn't the end.

Yeah, he liked the guys, and he really liked Blaine. Well, he'd been attracted to Blaine—he wasn't sure he knew him well enough yet to like him. He hoped to, though. Not that he needed a boyfriend at the moment, right? Now he needed to work, to focus on the science and find a job that would support his interests.

The guys all shouted out, "Hey! Blaine!" And Will added, "About fucking time, man. You're starving us to death."

"Mom needed me to help her with a few things. You know how it is." Blaine's hair was freshly washed and loose, the long mass wild and free now, making him look even thinner and more otherworldly than ever.

Flynn's body tightened, and he forced himself to ignore it. He got up with the others as they moved from the bar to a table. The guys all clapped Blaine on the shoulder, and Flynn offered his hand again; he wasn't one of the gang yet, not really. Not until they'd gone through a job together, he imagined.

That thing that had happened back when he'd first met Blaine rushed through him again as their skin made contact. Like a connection to the other side. Like something in him was responding to something in Blaine. Flynn swallowed and smiled, told himself to shake it off. He was a scientist, not a romantic; he needed to keep his head straight.

Flynn hadn't had anything to eat yet. That's what this was. He grabbed his menu, focused on it.

"I'm starving, guys," Blaine said. "Starving. Let's eat!"

Flynn had to smile—looked like he and Blaine were on the same wavelength.

"You're starving?" Jason shook his head. "We've been waiting for you to show up to eat, man. You don't get to pull the starving card now."

"Sorry to interrupt, guys, but are you ready to order?" a waitress asked, pen and pad in hand.

"I want a bacon cheeseburger, fries, and a Guinness, please." Blaine grinned, unapologetic as hell.

"I'll have the beef and Guinness stew," Flynn decided. "And what the hell, I'll have a Guinness too." God, he was famished. "Can I have some nachos, please?"

Darnell laughed, and Will shook his head. "Nice one. You want anything else?"

Flynn shook his head. "That should do me."

The other guys ordered, and everyone started talking, random snippets of conversation. Flynn sat back and watched, beginning to learn how they communicated.

Jason *was* the leader, no question, heading the conversation in different directions, making the best jokes, the wittiest comments.

Will was mostly quiet, putting in a few words here and there, while Darnell brayed with laughter on a regular basis.

Blaine watched, eyes wandering the crowd, searching.

Flynn found his own gaze following the same pathways, trying to find out what Blaine was looking for, what he'd seen.

He couldn't see anything out of the ordinary. Nothing at all. It was a bar and grill—mostly young, middle-class people out for a drink.

Flynn wondered how long the place had been here, what stories it held. Maybe that would explain what had Blaine's attention. Hell, maybe the guy was just checking the place out because he was tired and not into the conversation. Flynn didn't know. He really did need to learn these people.

"So, Blaine. How long have you seen spirits?"

"My whole life. I don't remember ever not seeing them, I guess."

"Cool. Was it scary at first?" It hadn't been for Flynn, though he'd never *seen* his mother, only felt her presence. It had been comforting that first time, not scary.

"No. No, it wasn't scary until I got older, I think. It took me a long time to sense my first malevolent spirit."

"Yeah? Were you trying to feel one? Or, I mean, waiting for it to happen? Or was it a shock?"

"It was a shock." Blaine shrugged and gave him a sheepish grin. "I got better at it."

"I can't decide if it would be easier to know or not to know. I mean, if you know it's there, you can try and defend against it. But if you don't know it's there, you're not scared. And will it hurt you if you don't know it's there? I'm guessing yes." Flynn shrugged. "Sorry, I don't mean to interrogate you."

"You're the scientist. I assume that means data, right?"

Flynn grinned and ducked his head. "Yeah, I guess that's how I operate." He did like to get as much information as possible before he made any kind of decision.

"Then that's cool. We want to be as thorough as possible. We can't get a TV deal if we aren't professional about this."

"Is that the goal?" Flynn didn't need to be a TV star. He just wanted to prove that ghosts were real. He hadn't thought much beyond that, honestly.

"It's where we can get funding, huh? At some point, my folks want this to be something more than a hobby if I'm gonna keep doing it."

Flynn chuckled. "You mean they want you to be able to support yourself? Shocking." He gave Blaine a wink. Truth was, he'd love to have parents who bugged him about what he was doing with his life.

"Yeah. Dad's losing patience. Fast."

"I'm sorry. You're helping out at home, though, aren't you? I mean if you worked a 'regular' job, you wouldn't be able to be there for them while your mother's going through this."

"Yeah. Totally. I run the store, and I help out at the farm, but… you know. Dad's a farmer, salt of the earth. Work at dawn, crash at dusk. No ghost chasing."

"Unless it's bringing in cash, huh? Well, hopefully we'll get a deal, then, and he can relax and let you be."

"It'll happen. We just have to do honest work."

"I'm all about data and tracking everything, doing it right." God, he was a dork too, talking about shop when they were out for supper so they could all get to know each other better. Which he'd already done with the other guys while they were waiting for Blaine. "So are you dating?" Christ, that was subtle. And possibly not entirely appropriate, either.

"Nope. I'm not really looking for someone at the moment. Things are so busy, so weird."

"Yeah. 'I see ghosts' makes for a good movie, but not a good opening line, eh?" Flynn got that. He'd learned to keep the fact that he believed in ghosts, had in fact had firsthand experience with them, to himself. His aunt hadn't wanted to know, and, it turned out, neither had his lovers.

"Not as a rule," Blaine agreed. "I'm already the hippie-dippy weirdo with the farm stand."

"Some people like that type." Flynn didn't have a type. Well, aside from guys of course, but he'd dated all sorts.

"It's a rarefied type, for sure."

"Some of us like unique and weird and rarefied. We're all here for the ghost hunting, after all. Normal isn't exactly our thing, huh?" Was he flirting? He didn't think so, but he couldn't seem to stop this line of questioning.

"I like that, man. That totally works for me."

Flynn smiled, but before he could say anything else, their waitress came back with his nachos, and Flynn's mouth actually watered. God, he was starving.

"Help yourselves, guys," he offered.

They all dug in, the chips and salsa flying fast and free.

Flynn got enough of it to assuage his hunger until his stew showed up, but man, he was going to have to remember that these guys could eat and could eat with speed.

He had a few sips of his Guinness, licking the foam from his lips.

For a second, Blaine's eyes caught his. He stared, their gazes locked. The moment seemed to build, to stretch between them.

Oh. Okay. That was… surprisingly hot.

And short-lived as Darnell banged him on the shoulder. "I said, did you want another beer?"

"Did you?" Flynn shook his head. "No, I think I'm good for now."

"Good deal. Blaine?"

"I'm good."

"Spoilsports." Darnell laughed and headed toward the bar.

"He likes his beer, huh?" Flynn chuckled. He couldn't be that much older than Darnell, but it sure felt like he was.

Blaine nodded. "He handles it better than anyone I've ever met, man. I can have two, maybe three, and I'm toast."

"Yeah? I'm a cheap date too," he admitted.

"No worries. We always have a designated driver."

"Oh yeah? That's good to know."

The waitress came again, this time with food for everyone, and they all dug in. Stew and burgers, french dip—everything smelled like heaven, and his stew tasted amazing.

Flynn ate bite after bite, scooping it up with the slices of crusty bread that came with it. He moaned happily over the rich and flavorful stew.

"Is it good? Can I try a bite?" Blaine asked.

"It's delicious." He dipped a corner of the bread into the stew and offered it to Blaine.

"Thank you. You rock." Blaine offered some french fries in return.

"Fair trade." Flynn grabbed the fries and snarfed them up. Not bad. He could see why the guys hung out here regularly. The food was *good*.

"Are you excited about going out with us this weekend? You nervous?"

"Yes, to both. I don't know what to expect, how to work with you guys, so there's some nerves. But this will be my first outing ghost hunting, so yeah, I'm very excited."

"We're going to this old hospital. We've gone a couple times already, just to scope it out."

He sat forward, his full attention on Blaine. "You get anything interesting?"

"A couple of EMF spikes. Nothing serious. Not yet."

"So you didn't see anyone? And that's normal? Does it take time for the ghosts to... trust you?"

"I don't know. Sometimes it's quick, sometimes it takes time. What I do isn't a science at all, man."

"You gonna mind if I take notes and observe and possibly make some correlations?" It was kind of what he did.

"It's sort of your job, right? This is what we need from you."

Chuckling, he nodded. "I was just thinking that exactly." He found himself grinning at Blaine, loving that they were in sync.

"Rock on. We'll do a trial run on Friday, see how things work, and then film on Saturday."

"I've got my equipment ready, and I can't wait." Flynn knew it was going to be a lot of hurry up and wait, but he was still excited to get started.

"Me either. Maybe we'll get some readings, something." Blaine shrugged. "At least we have permission to be there."

"Do you break into places a lot?" They didn't really want to get arrested for trespassing.

"No. Sometimes. No, not lots."

"Good to hear." He snagged another bite of bread.

"Yeah. We go for legal and reasonable. We're all legit."

"I know." Flynn had looked them up before applying for the job, after all.

Blaine pinked. "Sorry, I think I'm just really defensive tonight. Ignore me. Maybe I ought to have another beer."

"Something happen to put you on edge?" Flynn hoped it wasn't him—they'd had a good connection so far, and he was pretty sure they'd all been happy to have him join the team, Blaine included. He didn't think they'd been blowing smoke up his ass.

"Fight with my dad. Nothing serious—same old shit."

"Sorry to hear that. Hey, we could share a dessert. Sweet things can be very cathartic. As long as it's not chocolate, because then you're on your own." Flynn didn't like chocolate at all. He knew that made him some sort of freak. He wasn't very fond of bacon either, which probably made him an even bigger freak.

"You allergic?"

He shook his head. "I just don't like the stuff," he admitted, waiting for the shock, followed by the mocking.

"Huh. I don't like mint, so I get it. I'm not allergic or anything. I just don't like it."

Flynn had to grin. He swore he liked Blaine better every second. "A lot of people have random stuff they don't like, but most of them don't get not liking chocolate." He grabbed the little drinks-and-dessert booklet that was propped up at the side of the table against the metal condiments stand and began perusing it.

"I like it okay, but my thing is pastries. I love flaky bread stuff."

"Yeah? They've got a cheesecake wrapped in a deep-fried tortilla on the menu here. You wanna share? Not that we need to share a dessert or anything. You can totally have your own. I just know there's no way I'm going to want the whole thing to myself." He didn't have a big enough sweet tooth for that.

"Why not? We'll give it a try."

Darnell laughed, bumped shoulders with him. "Our Blaine's easy."

Flynn tried to ignore the little voice in his head that nudged him and waggled its eyebrows at him over that. Darnell had not meant easy like that, and Flynn was here for business, not fucking.

He waved the waitress over, willing his cheeks not to heat, and pointed to the decadent deep-fried tortilla cheesecake thing. "One of these with the caramel sauce to share, please."

"Sure thing, anyone else want dessert?"

"Hell yes." Darnell ordered the apple pie a la mode, while Jason got the Death by Chocolate cake, and Will asked for the peanut-butter cheesecake.

And Darnell asked for another round of beers, despite the fact he'd brought himself and Will another round from the bar. Flynn didn't say no, though. Now that'd he'd eaten, and quite a bit at that, he should be fine with another beer. Besides, his hotel was around the corner, so he didn't have to worry about driving.

"Are you going to get up and sing when they start karaoke tonight, Blaine?"

"Shut up, Will."

Flynn looked around. He hadn't noticed the karaoke setup hidden in the corner until Will had mentioned it, but he'd be damned if it wasn't there. "You sing?" he asked Blaine. He had a passable voice himself, though he tended only to sing while he worked.

Blaine's cheeks were bright red, but Will nodded. "He's good. You have to get him a little lubed up, but people love to hear him."

"Just another worthless talent," he muttered, and Jason frowned.

"Hey! Stop it, huh? You got this. Your dad's just super stressed- out right now, and you know it."

"Does singing make you happy?" Flynn asked quietly. When Blaine nodded, he added, "So that makes it a good thing, right? And you've got another beer coming, so we've got lubed up handled. Plus, I'm people, so I'd love to hear you."

Will laughed at his tease but nodded. "You can't deny Flynn the pleasure of listening to you and watching you emote up there on the stage."

"Shut up, guys." Blaine was going to catch on fire any second from the looks of it. Seriously.

"Do we need him to have that beer that's on its way before we really put on the pressure?" Flynn asked.

Jason nodded. "Probably. And if that doesn't work, we can always drag him up there. We outnumber him."

Darnell made this great hooting sound—sort of like a huge owl. "We can be his backup!"

"I'll join you after I've had a chance to watch a song or two." Flynn didn't want to miss it by being onstage with them. He had a hunch this was going to be a real treat. Too bad he only had the camera on his phone to document it with, but that would do in a pinch. He'd bet there was equipment in their van, though. It made him wonder if ghost hunters got mad if you used their equipment for non-ghost-sighting purposes.

His thoughts were disrupted by the arrival of their desserts, and Flynn had to stare. Every plate was huge. They probably all could have eaten off a single plate and been happy with that, and he was very glad that the tortilla cheesecake wasn't his alone. It looked amazing, but it also looked like it could feed a family with ten kids.

He offered a fork and the steak knife the dessert came with to Blaine. "Why don't you get us started?" He would nibble in around the edges, because now that his supper had had a chance to settle, he wasn't feeling very hungry anymore. Plus he had the Guinness to finish, and it was a heavy, hearty beer.

"Are you sure, man?"

He nodded, and Blaine cut into it, moaning softly as he took the first creamy bite.

Oh fuck. That was the sexiest thing Flynn had seen in a long time, and he couldn't help but wonder what that moan would sound like if it was because of a touch. His touch. *Stop that*, he told himself. *Stop it right now.* This was a brand-new gig. A whole new thing. He didn't need to fucking complicate—

Blaine took another bite and licked his lips.

Biting back his groan, Flynn looked away, ordering his prick to behave. Maybe he shouldn't finish that last beer.

"Your turn." Blaine pushed the plate over with a grin. "It's good.

"Yeah, I gathered that." He couldn't help grinning as he pulled the plate over toward him.

"I'm a sucker for sweets. What can I say?"

Flynn cut himself a piece and ate it, his eyes half closing at the taste. Damn, that really was groan-worthy. He licked his lips and nodded. "It's damn good."

"See? I don't lead you wrong, man."

"No, you don't. I'll be sure to remember that when we're out on a job." He ate another piece, the flavor sweet and creamy, the caramel rich and yummy. Okay, add that to the beer and he was in heaven.

Utter heaven.

The only thing that would make it better would be if he was going home with Blaine.

He blinked at himself. *Stop that.*

Flynn didn't even know where home for Blaine was, for God's sake. With his parents, he assumed. He took a breath and shoved another hunk of the delicious dessert into his mouth. Friends and coworkers. That's what they were becoming here.

He had a couple more bites, then passed the dessert back. "You'd better get some more or you'll miss out completely.

"One more. Maybe two." Blaine laughed and scooped up a bunch of whipped cream. "This is the best part."

No, Flynn thought maybe the best part was watching Blaine suck the whipped cream off his fingers. Just damn. It was hard to behave when Blaine did things like that.

"Drink your beer, Blaine man! George is setting up. You can sing 'Sugar' first."

Flynn grinned. "You've got a whole routine, do you?" he teased.

"I don't. I really don't." Blaine pinked. "I just like to sing."

"I'm just teasing. I'm looking forward to it. Honestly."

"Yeah, yeah. I'll go see how he's doing."

"Oh dude. He's totally going to sing." Darnell looked pleased as fuck about that.

Flynn turned to watch, and Blaine was as pretty going as he was coming. Lean but muscular, and that long hair was cool as fuck. And such a delicious-looking bubble butt.

He and the guys pulled all the chairs so they were facing the little stage, and Jason nudged him. "Don't tease him too hard because then it's forever before he sings again, but he's really good."

"I wouldn't, man. No way." After all, Blaine was the front man, right? He had to be something of an entertainer.

"Good man." Darnell patted him on the shoulder, and Flynn guessed he was slightly drunk.

Will had had about twice as much as Darnell but wasn't nearly as drunk. Strong constitution; good to know.

Some pretty girl got onstage and sang a Taylor Swift song. Then it was Blaine. Flynn sat slightly forward, watching and waiting with anticipation.

The Maroon 5 song started, and... shit, they were right. Blaine could sing. His falsetto was high and clear, the notes on pitch. Cool.

Smiling, Flynn tapped his hand on the table and nodded his head along to the beat. There was something very sexy about Blaine as he sang. Blaine was a natural up there, singing hard, laughing softly in between choruses.

Flynn began clapping along with the next chorus, Blaine's happiness infectious.

"See? He's good. He's really good, huh?" Will clapped and danced, obviously into it.

"He's fantastic. If he ever wants to give up ghost hunting, I bet he could make money singing." Flynn didn't get why Blaine's dad wouldn't be supportive of this voice.

"Until he sees a ghost midsong and freaks out."

"Oh man, has that happened?" That would be embarrassing enough here. Flynn could only imagine what it would be like if Blaine was on a big stage in front of a lot of people. It was one thing to be a ghost hunter with a TV show, quite another to be a singer and see ghosts. People would think he was crazy.

He'd never thought about that—about how awkward it had to be to sense things that most people didn't believe in. It wasn't the same for him. He'd felt his mother's presence and other stuff when he'd been trying, but he didn't suddenly have apparitions appearing in front of him.

That would be weird as hell, wouldn't it? To see some random ghost, some random person.

Flynn wondered how real the ghosts looked. Were they ephemeral, or were they more solid? Was it different with every ghost? Because if they looked solid, how would you know they were ghosts and not just other people? God, so many questions. So much to learn.

He couldn't wait to go out on their first hunt and get some answers.

The song came to an end, and Flynn clapped along with everyone else. It had been neat, but he had to admit, he had lost interest in favor of the ghosts. He was a little too focused, maybe. But that was who he was. Finding proof of ghosts, of the supernatural, of spirits—it was his life. Proving that his mother was still with him and not simply living on in his memories.

All the rest was a distraction.

Blaine sat down with a plop. "How'd I do?"

Will sat next to Blaine and put his arm around Blaine's shoulders. "Awesome as always, man. Awesome as always."

Flynn grinned and nodded. "That was pretty cool. And I think you were being modest. You've got a great singing voice."

"Thanks. I have fun goofing off."

"Well, if that's you goofing off, I can't wait to see what you do when you're serious." Flynn decided this was going to be a good gig, that these guys were legit.

All in all, he was glad he was here.

Chapter Three

"**MEL** Meter, EMF, Boo Bear—do we have the voice box? Cameras all charged? Backup batteries?" Lord, Jason was ramped up. Blaine hadn't heard that tone in his voice since they'd broken down over a train track.

Weird.

"You okay, buddy?" he asked. Hopefully it was just nerves with Flynn starting tonight.

"I'm fine," Jason snapped. "Why does everyone keep asking me that?"

Will snorted. "Because you're micro-fucking-managing. Of course the equipment is all here, in good working order, and charged up. I know how to do my goddamned job." There wasn't a ton of heat in the words, but Will shot Jason a look that said he wasn't going to put up with much more of Jason's crap.

Flynn came out of the hotel he was staying at, a backpack on and carrying two bags. Darnell opened the door for him. "Hey, guys, thanks for the lift."

"Sure. Anytime." They were all still staring at Jason, wide-eyed.

Flynn looked around as he set his bags on the far back seat. "Everything okay?"

Will shrugged. "Fine and fucking dandy."

"Seems like everyone's edgy today. I'm going to burn sage in the van again if everyone isn't careful." Blaine knew that threat would work like a charm.

"I said I'm fine!" Jason all but shouted.

Flynn's eyes went wide, and he very carefully, quietly, put his seat belt on.

Blaine moved to the seat next to Jason and reached out, touching Jase's arm. "Sorry, man. I was just messing with Sasquatch."

"You know what happens to people who do that."

"Messing with the Sasquatch?" Flynn asked. "I thought we were hunting ghosts."

"God. Tell me you're not an anti-TV guy. I love those beef jerky commercials."

"I'm not anti-TV. I just don't have a lot of time for it. I tend to binge-watch shows on Netflix or Hulu if I've got the downtime. Like right after exams. I'm not sure yet when my downtime is going to be...."

"Ah. Well, it's a stupid commercial, but I love them." And Blaine was a dipshit who hadn't finished college.

"Yeah, they're pretty funny," Darnell put in. "And it's kind of like poking the bear—you just shouldn't do it."

"So in this scenario, Jason's the Sasquatch, and you were poking him? Which sounds way dirtier than I meant it." Flynn laughed.

Jason blinked, and there was a second where it was either going to go good or bad, and then Jase cracked up, the tension easing with a pop Blaine could feel.

Flynn had to have felt it too, because he relaxed visibly. "So guys, my gaydar isn't the greatest, so pardon the question, but do we all play for the same team here?"

"Assuming you mean are we queer, then yes. Totally. All of us. If not, then I have no idea." Blaine winked at Flynn. His gaydar was great.

"No, that's exactly what I meant. I was pretty sure, but I knew if I assumed, I could say something at some point that offended someone. I try not to, but damn, I can put my foot in my mouth sometimes."

"I hear that's a kink," Darnell drawled.

"That's just gross, man." Will punched Darnell in the shoulder. "Thanks for the image."

Flynn just laughed. "Hobbit feet are gross, but most guys have decent feet. Not that I'm advocating sucking toes or anything. Of course I'm not disadvocating for it, either."

"I don't want to think about toe sucking before we ghost hunt," Blaine said.

"Have you seen ghosts doing it before?" Flynn asked, like the question had only just occurred to him.

"No. No, you know, I haven't." Blaine blinked. "I mean, I guess you're not horny as a ghost."

"I don't know, man. I've never been one." Flynn winked at him. "But have you seen lover ghosts? I mean, two together who were together when they were still alive?" Flynn's eyes were alight, bright with curiosity.

"I don't know. Maybe. You know, it's really intense and fast." And Blaine had worried that he was crazy.

"Do you usually debrief after? Tell the guys what you saw and document it?" Flynn certainly didn't seem to think Blaine was crazy.

"God, no," Jason said. "We go to bed, and Blaine goes right to work on Saturday mornings."

Yeah. That was the deal. Blaine stocked and opened the farm stand Saturday morning and didn't bitch. By the time Sunday rolled around, he was sound asleep in the van.

"You don't document anything?" Flynn sounded shocked. "Are you gonna fight me on changing that? I mean how do you…? What…? I just…. You need to document everything, you absolutely do. Or at least I do."

"Document away."

"Listen to his exhausted ramblings, huh?" Jason chuckled and shook his head. "If Blaine lets you, go for it."

"Good, good. It's an important part of the process. I mean, don't you guys analyze what you find and stuff? Surely you do."

"We all have other jobs right now. Lives. We keep all our recordings, but Jill took care of that for the most part," Blaine explained. "That was part of her job."

"So I basically get carte blanche for setting this end of stuff up how I want, eh?" Flynn rubbed his hands together and gave a maniacal little laugh. "Just kidding. I swear I'm not power hungry."

"That reminds me. You'll have to stop over and get all the film and audio from the barn. I have the most storage space, you know?" He lived in a restored barn on his folks' farm, and it was huge and drafty and amazing.

"Oh cool! But it's going to have to wait until I find a place to live." Flynn sounded so disappointed.

"You looking to rent a place or buy?" He could totally use the bonus cash that a roommate could bring, not to mention the company.

"Probably rent to start with. I need to save up if I'm going to be buying. You'll have to tell me where the quiet neighborhoods are."

"Shit, man," Darnell said. "Rent that cool-assed room in Blaine's barn."

Flynn shot him a look. "Yeah? You've got space going? You don't have to rent to me just because I'm ghost hunting with you, but I'd be interested if you are. Is this the same barn where all your footage is stored? Because that would be handy."

"Yeah. I renovated one of the barns—two thousand square feet of drafty wonder." And he loved it.

"Oh, very cool. Are there any residents aside from you?"

Flynn didn't have to spell out that he meant ghosts.

"Not that I've ever seen, thank goodness."

"No? You wouldn't want a benevolent otherworldly neighbor?" Flynn asked. "Because I totally would."

"Benevolent would be great if you knew for sure."

"You can't tell, eh? There isn't like... an aura around them?" Flynn seemed fascinated by it all.

Blaine wasn't sure what he was supposed to say.

Flynn waited patiently but clearly expected an answer. He was so damn good-looking, a handsome face, a great body.... Quite a distraction.

Blaine shook himself. "It's not like I always *see* these full-bodied apparitions. I sense them more than anything."

"But like you said before, it's freakier *not* seeing them."

"Exactly." It felt kind of good to have someone get it.

"You guys ever picked up apparitions on any of the equipment?" Flynn was just a ball of curiosity, but it was probably good, having someone look at how they did things, maybe bring in some new ideas.

"Couple of spirit balls and some kickass EMF readings," Blaine replied.

"That's great! I'm really hoping to get some stuff on camera. Being able to actually see things is about the only thing some people will believe. Of course, nowadays it's easy enough to fake that kind of thing if you know what you're doing, so I'm not sure even that'll do anymore." Flynn laughed a little dryly. "Some people will always find ways to shake other people down."

"It's easier not to believe, isn't it? Isn't that easier?"

"I guess. If you haven't had any experience with it. I mean, given what you feel, would it be easier to ignore it and not believe?"

"No. Then you just think you're insane." And that was always Blaine's worry. Always.

"Dude, you're not insane." Flynn sounded pretty sure of that. "And we're going to prove it."

"There's a fast-food joint up ahead," Will told them from the driver's seat. "This is our last chance to stop before we get to the hospital, and I do believe we are SOL there when it comes to the amenities."

Blaine leaned toward the speaker. "Double bacon cheeseburger, large fries, Coke, and some chicken nuggets for me."

Flynn put in his order. "I'll have two extra-large fries and a vanilla milkshake, please."

Darnell and Jason both wanted cheeseburgers and fries with Cokes, and they all passed money over to Will as he pulled into the drive-through.

Flynn grinned at Blaine as they waited. "So, you really want a roommate?"

"Sure, if you're willing. I can always use the extra cash."

"How much are we looking at? I've got a budget, so I know how much I can spend on living expenses and I figure rooming with someone will be cheaper than forging out on my own."

"You want to say two fifty a month? You can share the kitchen, and you'll have your own bathroom," Blaine noted.

"That sounds more than reasonable—are you sure that'll cover utilities and everything? I'll be running my computer pretty much full-time."

"We'll see, huh? If it's more, it'll just be twenty bucks or so, right?"

"I have no clue, but revisiting it after you start getting bills sounds good. Are you much of a cook? I do okay in the kitchen. I mean, I know how long it takes to cook most meats and I can roast potatoes and vegetables with the best of them."

Blaine shrugged. "I can make basic stuff—farm food, you know? When Mom's healthy, she cooks a ton."

"You say farm food like it's subpar or something. I'm a meat and potatoes guy—so I'm down with that. Maybe we can trade off cooking? You know, rather than both trying to get our own stuff done. When I had roommates at school, I hated the whole compartmentalized food thing. If I'm cooking a pot of pasta, doesn't it make sense to make it for everyone? It doesn't exactly take extra time or effort to make two portions instead of one."

"Sure. Sure, why not? I mean, we'll see if our schedules mesh."

"Sounds great." Flynn grabbed his shake and fries as they were passed back, opened a bunch of the little ketchup packages, and poured them into the bags of fries.

Blaine scarfed down his burger, making yummy noises that were damn near perverse, even if he did say so himself.

Flynn kept shooting him looks, and he fought to shut up. "Sorry, it's so good."

"No, no, you're good. I mean, go for it. Those are great sounds, that's all." Flynn gave him a sheepish grin. "Sorry for staring."

"Eh. I'm just starving. It was too busy to eat today, somehow." He'd been running his ass off, getting ready for Saturday morning.

"Ah, that's how you stay so thin." Flynn munched on a ketchup-covered fry, then licked the salt and tomato off his fingers.

It was Blaine's turn to find himself staring.

Okay, pretty. He did like eye candy.

"You do make great noises when you eat, though," Flynn told him between mouthfuls and more licking. "I noticed that the other night at the pub."

"Yeah?" Okay, he needed to watch that, because how embarrassing.

"Yeah." Flynn didn't say anything else, but the expression on his face said it was a good thing, and Flynn's eyes danced with an expression of…. Blaine didn't know—it didn't feel like he was being laughed at, though.

Whatever it was, it was. He just focused on his chicken and on not making any noise.

"We've got another half hour or so," Will told them as they turned off the highway and onto a smaller road. The sun was nearly down now, the atmosphere becoming more mysterious, spooky.

Blaine knew that Jason had chosen this venue to test Flynn. It was creepy as fuck but familiar to them, and they'd had better than average luck in the building.

It didn't hurt that they knew the owners.

Flynn rubbed his hands together. "I gotta admit, I'm looking forward to it. I want to get started."

"I hope you have fun. Hell, I hope we get some good readings, something." Last time they'd had a few EMF spikes that were pretty damn cool.

"God yes." Flynn was almost bouncing, throwing him a grin. "You're going to have to tell me everything you see and feel. Everything."

"You got it. I promise, man. I'll give it up."

"Huh?" Jason looked up, his eyes going wide. "You're giving it up? To Flynn? Did I hear right?"

Will snorted, and Darnell cackled. Jason was notorious for being in his own head and only catching a small part of any conversation.

Flynn didn't miss a beat, though, nodding vigorously. "You heard right—he totally said exactly that."

"Huh?" Jason looked at him, then pursed his lips. "Yeah, no."

"I expect you all to," Flynn said, making Will sputter from the front seat.

Darnell clapped his hands. "You heard it here first, folks!"

Jason's mouth dropped open as he stared.

Flynn laughed, eyes twinkling. "Seriously, though. I'm going to want updates from all of you on what you're seeing, how you're feeling. What kinds of readings you're getting. I need all the data I can collect and then some in order to draw any conclusions about our findings."

"I thought you joining us was supposed to make it less work for the rest of us, not more," complained Darnell.

"None of our conclusions will be worth a damn if we don't have data to back it up," Flynn insisted.

"He's joining us because he's got cred."

"No experience, though," Jason noted with a grin that said he knew he was being a bitch and was doing it on purpose.

Flynn stuck his tongue out at Jason. "Told you I'm a fast learner. Hopefully I'll be able to limit my questions to what you're all experiencing rather than how things work."

"That's why we're doing this run, man. Training." Blaine offered Flynn a grin that he hoped was friendly and warm.

"Cool. Cool." Flynn finished his milkshake, and Blaine told himself to stop perving on the guy's suction.

He needed to get laid. Maybe Darnell would be willing to do joint hand jobs. Darnell was between guys. That might be awkward at his place with Flynn there, though. But Darnell had his own place, and there was always the van. It wouldn't be the first time it had been used for something other than hauling people and equipment from point A to point ghost.

They turned onto a bumpy dirt road, and Blaine knew they were almost there.

"Hold on to your butts, guys."

Flynn cackled, but he grabbed hold of the handle above the door with one hand and Blaine's leg with the other as they flew over their first bump. "Fuck!" Flynn's fingers dug into Blaine's thigh.

"Not quite, but it's a rush, huh?"

"Unexpected." Flynn laughed. "Good thing I like roller coasters."

"Me too!" Oh, they'd have to go. The others guys all hated them.

"Bonus! We'll have to hit the amusement park soon. I haven't been in a couple years."

They went over another bump, and Flynn cried out happily.

Blaine cracked up and grabbed his Coke as it tried to go over. Flynn hooted with him, and Jason shook his head.

"You guys are crazy."

"Probably goes with the territory," Flynn shot back, and this time it was Darnell who cracked up.

"No shit. Five gay ghost hunters in a shitty van!"

"Hey," growled Will. "The van is not shitty." He patted the dashboard. "He didn't mean it, darling. We think you're an amazing van, and we hope you last forever."

Blaine could see Flynn biting his lower lip, eyes twinkling like crazy.

"She is a stunning little van, Will, dear. Your soul mate."

Will raised his hand over the top of his seat, one finger up. "She's treated me better than any of my relationships has."

"Well, that's pretty sad," Flynn noted.

"That's fucking pitiful," Blaine added.

"Don't make me stop this van," Will said, sounding so much like Blaine's father when Blaine was young that he had to laugh.

Flynn sniggered as well, biting his lip, clearly trying not to laugh out loud.

"You guys are living dangerously," Darnell chided. "Seriously. It's not right to get between a man and his van."

They all burst out laughing at that, the van ringing with it. It was good, surrounding them with positive energy.

Jason leaned over and knocked shoulders with Blaine. "Sorry about earlier. Me and Darren…. He's cheating on me."

"Oh man."

"Yeah. Not common knowledge, but it's not you."

"Right." God, that sucked. Jase hadn't been with Darren for eons, but longer than a couple of months. Long enough that it had to hurt.

"I'm sorry," Flynn murmured. "I don't get cheating. If you want to be with someone else, man up and let the person you're with know it's over. It's still going to hurt, but it won't be a betrayal like cheating is. People suck."

"Right on." Blaine grabbed Jason's hand and squeezed. "So, we are totally finding spirits tonight. Or tomorrow. Totally."

"As a reward for being cheated on?" Jason asked, voice dry. Then he smiled. "That would work for me. Darren's an asshole for cheating, and I'd rather have ghosts than him."

"Yes. He's a fuckmonster."

"A fuckmonster?" Jason's lips twitched, and they all started laughing again. "I'm going to remember that for the next time I run into him."

They bounced across a couple of large dips in the road, and Flynn threw his hands up again and shouted out "Whoo!" This time Darnell and Jason joined him. Will, happily, did not.

Blaine leaned back, bouncing against the side of the van. He thought Flynn was going to fit in fine. Just fine.

They rounded a corner, and suddenly the decrepit hospital was in front of them, looming in the near darkness. It was spooky enough during the day, but at night the creep factor was pretty high.

Flynn bounced, without the aid of the van this time, and rubbed his hands together. "Oh man, I can hardly believe we're here and this is it. I've been waiting to do this forever."

Blaine chuckled softly, and Jase nodded, grinned. "Man, this is totally what we all needed. A shot of enthusiasm. I like it."

"I can't imagine this ever becoming old hat," Flynn admitted. "I mean, ghosts! What's not to be enthusiastic about?"

"Well, when you hit a bunch in a row that don't pan out, you start worrying." At least Blaine did.

"Ah, yeah. I can see where that would be hard." Flynn nodded as Will parked the van near the side of the building.

Will turned off the engine and leaned around to the back. "You gonna take Flynn on a walk-through while I get all the equipment set up?"

"Yeah. Yeah, come on. I'll give you the ten-cent tour." He hopped out of the van, the slight buzz that always seemed to herald a busy spirit night already ringing in his ears.

Flynn got out, bag in hand. "Can I bring my camera? I'll leave the rest of the stuff for Will, but I'd love to get some establishing shots as we go through the place."

"Go for it. We'll start in the lobby. Watch for nails." God knew he'd stepped on enough.

Flynn nodded and stomped his feet, his work boots loud. "Steel toed. I did my homework."

Blaine had a feeling Flynn had been a Boy Scout.

They went in, passing under the sign on the front of the building that should have read Eugene Thurston Memorial Hospital, but had enough letters missing that it actually read ug Thurst Mem Ho. It had cracked them all up when they'd first seen it. Blaine figured some kids had had fun with that one a while back. It was too perfect to be random.

"Okay, this is the lobby. The floors are solid, and we'll set up here at the counter. It's been abandoned since the eighties, so it's been empty a long time."

"Are there any horror stories associated with the place?" Flynn asked. "I mean, obviously people died here, but were any of them under mysterious or sinister circumstances?"

"There was a mass shooting in the emergency room in the early sixties. Eight people died. Four nurses, two doctors, and two patients."

"Wow. That's tragic." Flynn looked around, using his flashlight to check out the walls. "Is that where you've had hits? In the emergency room?"

"In the emergency room and one of the rooms upstairs—204."

"Yeah? Have you got a history for that room?" Flynn followed close behind Blaine, probably reacting to how eerie the place was with the only illumination from their flashlights.

"I don't." All he had was feelings. The feeling for 204 had been… creepy. Bad. Slick. Oily.

"Is it awful in the emergency room?" Flynn asked as they made their way there. "Like, are murdered ghosts worse?"

"To me it feels a little frantic." Rushed. He wasn't even sure they knew, if he was going to be honest.

"Frantic? Like they're still working the emergency room or something?" Flynn asked.

"Yeah, maybe? It's a little distant. We'll do some EMF work and ask." That would give Flynn some data, right?

"Sounds good." They got to the emergency room, and Flynn shivered. "Wow. Even if I hadn't known you'd found something, I'd think this would be the place to start. Or maybe I just feel it because you said there was something here. Don't tell me anything else, okay? Let me see if I feel anything on my own first."

Flynn swung the flashlight around, checking out the emergency room, shying away from the spot where two of the nurses and a doctor had been shot in a cluster. Interesting—Blaine hadn't told Flynn where anything had happened.

Neat.

He didn't worry about Flynn. No, he leaned against the nurses' station and closed his eyes, opening up to the whispers that seemed to float about him.

That frantic feeling hit him first. Not panic, just *hurry, hurry, don't just stand there, do something*. All he had to do was breathe and let the sensation happen. It would calm down.

"Oh man." Flynn gasped. "So much anger, right here."

Blaine opened his eyes to find Flynn standing near the old entrance doors, and he could see something around Flynn, an area that was darker and sort of shimmered.

A sudden rush of jealousy hit him, and he nudged it back. So what if he wasn't the only psychic, right?

Flynn shivered and moved away quickly. "I don't know. I couldn't see anything, but it felt…. Evil sounds so cheesy, you know?" Coming over to Blaine, Flynn touched his hand, clearly a little spooked.

"Not cheesy. Not at all." A mean part of him thought, *Maybe you can do the walk-through*, but he ignored it. He wasn't an asshole. He wasn't.

"Good. That was the only word I had for it." Flynn stepped closer again, and Blaine could feel his warmth. "I've never felt anything like that before. Just my mom. I don't know if it's real or if it's because of the atmosphere and knowing the murders happened here."

"Well, make sure you take notes on what you feel, huh?"

"Right, right. Do you usually take notes on the walk-through or just when you have all the equipment set up and it's official?" Flynn kept shining his flashlight around the place, but he wasn't leaving Blaine's side.

"When all the equipment is set up." Because his job was to be charming and dramatic, dammit.

"Cool." Flynn flashed his light several times at the spot where he'd felt the anger and also the area he'd avoided where the two nurses and a doctor had died, but he didn't seem to be able to see anything at either spot. "So where do we go from here?"

"I'll lead you through radiology. All the equipment is gone."

"Sure thing." Flynn put a hand on Blaine's back as they began to move, then drew it away. "Sorry. Sorry. I've got to admit, I'm a little more spooked than I expected to be."

"Oh man. I hear you. It's creepy the first time."

"How many times have you guys come here?" Flynn asked, staying close, but not actually holding on to him.

"This is number three. I mean, it's day five, but visit three, you know?"

"Right. Because some visits are more than one day only. Like this one. Checking it out tonight and setting up, doing most of the work tomorrow. Are we going to sleep in the van or at a nearby motel or something? It seems like a long way to go back and forth."

"Will can take me home to work, sleep in the van, and then drive me back here. You guys will share a motel room." It sucked, but it was the best solution. He had responsibilities.

"You've got to do stuff for your folks, eh? I can see the good and the bad in that."

They took the stairs in the middle of the place—these being in the best repair.

"Watch your step," Blaine warned. "There's no guarantees in here, you know?"

"Yeah, I get it. Something could give way at any moment after thirty years of no repairs or anything."

Flynn stayed close, and the stairs groaned and creaked, adding to the general spookiness of the atmosphere.

The whole creepy vibe helped Blaine be open to the spirits, helped him get into the right frame of mind for it. Even if nothing happened, he'd be able to make a show of it. When he had nerves, he did a better job.

They got upstairs, and he turned to the right, toward radiology.

"Jesus. How is it even darker up here?" Flynn asked.

"There's only windows in the rooms up here."

"Damn. It's spooky as hell."

"Yeah. I tell myself that there's nothing in the dark that isn't here in the light." But it was a lie.

"Do you believe yourself?" Flynn asked, hand finding Blaine's and slipping into it. There was a buzz, like he would have known that was Flynn's hand even if there'd been a dozen people who could have reached for him.

"No. Not really. Everything's spookier at night."

Flynn chuckled and squeezed his hand. "Somehow that makes me feel better."

"Yeah, well, two guys terrified out of their minds is better than being alone."

That made Flynn laugh louder, and the sound echoed weirdly, coming back as the laughter of madmen all around them. Flynn snapped his mouth closed.

"Dude, that was pretty cool." Blaine was all over that.

"Big echo, huh?" Flynn said very quietly.

"Huge. I wonder if we did that on tape if we'd hear something interesting."

"You think it wasn't just an echo of my voice?" Flynn asked, sounding like he was regaining his equilibrium.

"Who knows? You never can tell until you play the recordings." He never heard things as clearly as he did on the EVP.

"Awesome. I'm willing to cackle like an idiot again later." They got to radiology, noises coming from the dark, supposedly empty room. "What is that?"

"Mice." Blaine rolled his eyes. "Fucking mice."

"As long as they're mice and not rats, there's nothing scary about that." Flynn squeezed Blaine's hand, sending tingles shooting up his arm. Flynn apparently didn't plan on letting him go quite yet.

"No. No. I mean, I've seen lots of little mice, no sewer rats or tree rats or anything."

"Good. So what happened up here? Or is it that the X-ray machines and stuff make it easier to see the ghosts?"

"I haven't the foggiest. We got some cool EVPs up here, you know?" Sometimes things just happened. At least that was Blaine's experience.

"Cool." Flynn finally let go of his hand and prowled around the room, lighting the way with his flashlight, curious about everything.

This room was the least interesting visually—a series of large empty rooms—but they'd heard the best stuff up here.

Flynn walked along, taking everything in but not venturing too far from Blaine. "It really is spooky."

"Yeah." Blaine found this pretty low-key, though, comparatively.

Flynn finally shrugged. "I don't feel anything but the general creepiness, but that could be because it *is* pretty creepy, and that's superseding everything."

"It's a lot of smoke and mirrors and some kickass echoes, huh?" Blaine closed his eyes, the dust in the air tickling his nose and making him want to sneeze.

"Uh-huh. I can't wait to get up here with the instruments, see what we can measure."

"We'll have to try the laughter thing too. Just because it's new."

Flynn chuckled. "Who'd have thought me being a goofball would lead to a new thing?"

"You'd be surprised. Half of what we get is accidental."

"Damn. That is going to drive me crazy. On the other hand, a lot of great discoveries were accidents. One thing discovered while someone was trying to invent something completely different. Plus you learn more by failing than you do by succeeding. A lot of people don't know that about science. About how important failure really is." Flynn was clearly passionate about the subject. Blaine could hear it in his voice.

"In our line of work, failure just means a bad night on film."

"But that gives us something to go on for next time. I tell you, failure is a good thing. You'd never have any staying power, anyway, if it always went your way. You've learned to be patient and to not expect a dozen ghosts doing the safety dance when you show up."

"You're something else, man. This is going to be fun." Blaine believed that too. There was something about Flynn's raw enthusiasm that made Blaine ready to work.

"Is there anything else we should check out?" Flynn asked.

He thought about taking Flynn to room 204, then thought better of it. "No, this ought to be good enough for now. For tonight."

"You hesitated there for a second. Are you sure?" Flynn touched his arm again, little tingles spreading out from the spot where they connected.

"Yeah. Yeah, I'm sure. We'll just focus here tonight."

"Okay, cool." Flynn kept holding on to him as they headed back down the pitch-black hall to the stairs in the middle of the building. "I feel like laughing again to see if the echo is still there."

"Not until we have a recorder up here, man. That's too good to waste."

"Okay, okay. No laughing." There was laughter in Flynn's voice, though, as they headed carefully down the stairs.

"Shut up."

"You guys okay?" Will called.

Flynn jumped about a foot at Will's voice, his hand tightening on Blaine's arm. "Fuck, that scared the shit out of me."

"Remember, you're not alone, huh? Will, Jase, Darnell—" He paused. "—me."

"I hadn't forgotten about you," Flynn murmured, and this time the squeeze to his arm was clearly deliberate.

"No?" That felt too good, honestly.

"Not at all. And not just because we're together."

As they got to the bottom of the steps, Will came into view, glaring. "You should have answered when I called out. I was about to head up to make sure."

"Yes, Mother." Blaine let his eyes roll, all dramatic and playful. "You scared?"

"No," Will growled. "But what if something had happened to the two of you?" Will gave them each a walkie-talkie. "Next time take these with you."

"Promise." He clipped it onto his waistband. "We were together."

"Good. Nobody goes anywhere alone." Will wagged his finger at them. "And call me mother all you like, but we haven't lost anyone yet, and that's down to looking out for each other. Come on. I've got everything set up. We should test everything, and I'm betting you want to explore a room or two before we head out for the night."

"God yes. Let's not waste the time we have."

"Better come and check the equipment, then, and Darnell and I will start filming."

They followed Will back to the lobby where everything was set up, Flynn immediately checking the EMF readers and the thermal cameras.

Darnell and Jason were there, fooling with the cameras and double-checking the two laptops. They had a couple of new thermal recorders that were motion sensitive.

"Where do you want to set these bad boys up?" Jason asked.

"Let's put one in the ER and one up in"—*room 204*—"X-ray."

"Got it." Jason headed out.

Will growled after him, "Take Darnell with you, and have you got your walkies with you?"

Darnell rolled his eyes, showed Will his walkie-talkie, and headed off after Jason.

"Okay, who's playing cameraman for me today?"

"Me." Will raised his hand like he was in school. "That way Flynn can run the EMF and the infrared and the two of you can focus on the Paranormal Activity." Will always said it so that you could tell he was capitalizing it.

"Are you comfortable with being on camera, Flynn?"

"Yeah, that's fine. Besides, you'll get most of the attention from the thing." Flynn pocketed a pack of extra batteries. He gave Blaine a happy grin. "Ready and reporting for duty."

"Rock on." Blaine made sure his hair was smooth and braided, his shirt clean. "Okay, let's do this."

The light from the camera came on, and Blaine put on his best smile. "Welcome to the Eugene Thurston Memorial Hospital. I'm Blaine Franks, and with my buddies Flynn, Will, Jase, and Darnell, we're the Supernatural Explorers."

Flynn waved when Blaine got to him but didn't add anything as he already had the EMF reader turned on and was checking the readings.

"Let's do this thing!" Blaine said, and they headed in.

Flynn was all business now—no more rush of questions, his focus on the results he was getting with the EMF reader.

"We're going to check out the ER first. It was the scene of a mass shooting, shortly before the hospital closed, where eight people were killed." Blaine knew the more grisly details they could give, the better people would like it. "A shooter came in—Dave Underwood—looking for his ex-wife, Maryann. He ended up killing her and many of her coworkers, along with two patients and himself. Tonight we're going to try and communicate with them."

Out of the corner of his eye, he saw Flynn grinning and bouncing. It felt good having that positive and enthusiastic energy there. It made Blaine feel like maybe they weren't wasting their time on a fool's errand.

They made their way down the hall, stopping about halfway along when Flynn made a noise. "We're getting a high reading, here by the admin offices." Flynn moved the EMF reader around, and Blaine peered over his shoulder at the device. The needle was jumping like crazy.

"Let's try an EVP." Blaine turned on the recorder. "Is there anyone here with us? Maryann? Are you here?"

Flynn switched on the infrared camera and aimed it in the direction where the EMF reader had pinged. "Ask again," Flynn suggested quietly.

"Maryann? Are you here with us? Do you have anything you'd like to say to us?" Blaine paused, giving the spirits a chance to respond. "Anything at all?"

There was a lot of creaking and groaning, but it sort of sounded more like the building settling than noises a spirit might make.

"You feeling anything?" Flynn asked, almost whispering.

"Not so far. But let's keep running the EVP, huh?" Blaine closed his eyes, took a deep breath. "Is there anyone who wants to speak to us? Just talk into the recorder."

Will and Flynn stayed silent. In fact, Blaine could almost hear them holding their breath.

Then Flynn spoke quietly. "I've got something on the infrared. Just shadows, but they suddenly appeared, and they're moving toward you."

Fuck. "If you need to speak to me, I'm right here."

"One of them is responding to you. Keep talking." Flynn took a couple of steps in his direction. Blaine didn't know if it was for his benefit or Flynn's.

"Tell us what you need to say. Speak right into the recorder."

Flynn nodded and pointed to the ghostly figure on the infrared camera. It didn't look like a person, but it was vaguely human shaped—the right height and width, even if there was no definition to it.

Blaine let the recorder run, trying as hard as he could not to either move or freak out.

The thing came closer, still visible only on the special camera. He couldn't see anything with his naked eye. The air got cold, the drop in temperature sudden, and the image on the infrared sharpened. It was right there in the foreground now, almost on top of them.

Flynn began breathing rapidly, quick little pants that all of a sudden became visible, the air cold enough that each exhalation showed.

Then he blinked, eyes huge, and poof. The moment was gone. Disappeared.

Flynn's cheer was quiet, but it was there, and Blaine could feel the excitement pouring from him. "That was so cool. Could you see anything? With the naked eye, I mean."

Blaine shook his head. "No. Nothing. I felt the temperature drop. Did we get a reading?"

"Yeah. The EMF was going nuts, and you saw the thing on the infrared camera. It got damn cold there for a minute." Flynn's excitement was contagious. Even Will was chuckling.

"Rock on. Hopefully we'll have some EVP too." Damn. Damn, that had been cool.

Flynn nodded, still bouncing on the balls of his feet like a big kid.

"Let's keep going," muttered Will. "The ER's just ahead."

"Good deal. We're heading into the emergency room proper now. We've just experienced some cold spots and a measurable visual on our infrared cameras, so we're very hopeful that Maryann will continue to try and reach out to us."

"A lot of people died in the emergency room," Flynn added. "We could hit on more than just Maryann." He was back to using the EMF detector, the little handheld machine beeping along happily but not showing anything significant yet.

"Sure. Go ahead. Call away." What the actual fuck? Blaine was supposed to lead the team, right? At least in this? Right? "I'm going to take a break. You keep filming, Flynn, huh?" He needed to calm the fuck down and quit being a prima donna. Seriously.

"What?" Flynn and Will said it together, Will actually lowering the camera to look at him.

"Did I do something wrong?" Flynn asked. "I didn't mean to—this is all so new, you know?"

"Not at all." He cleared his throat dramatically. "I need to grab a bottle of water. Keep filming. We'll cut me back in."

"Okay." Flynn looked concerned but didn't question him. "We'll wait for you here."

Will had one eyebrow up and a questioning look in his eyes, but he didn't say anything.

Blaine waved once and jogged toward the others. There'd be a cooler with bottles of water. Hell, maybe he'd run outside and take a leak and just focus. It was never going to be seamless, adding a new person to the group. Maybe he'd become complacent. Maybe that's why they sucked.

Jason and Darnell had returned from setting up the motion-activated cameras and were checking the feeds when he got back to the lobby.

"Hey, Blaine," Jason said. "You guys forget something?"

"Just need a drink. Throat's dry. They're still filming."

Flynn might be your new psychic after all.

Darnell tossed him a water bottle. "You'd better get back there. They need you."

"They're fine. I may take a handheld and a Mel Meter, head upstairs real quick and get some readings."

Darnell snorted. "You camera shy all of a sudden?"

Jason didn't say anything but was watching him, looking as surprised as Darnell.

"Shit no. Flynn wants to try some stuff. I thought I'd give him his head."

"You're the front man. If I wanted Flynn to do it, I'd have told you." Jase's voice was sure, firm. "You get your ass in front of the camera and show everyone how it's done. You're the one with the spark."

He opened his mouth to retort, but before he could, the walkies crackled.

"Blaine, man, you coming back soon?" Will asked. "We're waiting on you to go into the ER, and there's a bunch of spooky noises and a lot of action on the EMF reader."

"Aka get your ass back there squared," Jase said, pointing toward the hall.

Blaine laughed as he ran back. Yeah, he was a dipshit. An emotional dork.

The guys were waiting for him, and they both cheered as he got there, Flynn immediately showing him the EMF reader. "Look at this! There's a ton of activity, and I swear to God it feels like it's way colder in there. Will said he feels it too."

Will grunted. "Definitely something going on in there that needs your touch, man."

"Okay. Okay, well, you guys back off a little and let me focus." If he was going to do this, he needed to trust in it, right? Of course right.

Blaine closed his eyes and relaxed, listening as Will and Flynn moved back. The sound was sure and sharp for a second. Then it faded as they stilled.

He swore he could feel their warmth behind him, contrasting strongly with the decidedly cooler air in front of him. They stayed quiet and still, though, letting him do his thing.

"If you want to talk to me, I'm listening."

"No, you're not."

The words were low but solid. Not the fuzzy whispering he was used to.

"I am. I'm right here. Tell me what you need."

Nothing.

Nothing.

"Room 204."

That wasn't a voice. It was a thought. Still, he wasn't ready to share that.

Flynn took a gasping breath but didn't say anything.

"Blaine? We going to go in there?" Will asked, voice soft but not a whisper. Whispers could be fucking creepy in situations like this.

"What? Go in where?" He hadn't said anything about 204.

"The bay where the shootings happened."

"Huh? Yeah. Yeah, sure. Did you guys hear anyone answer me?"

"Yes," Flynn and Will answered at the same time.

"Hopefully it'll come through on the camera's audio," Will added.

"Good deal." So he wasn't crazy, which was handy. "Come on. Let's try in the bay."

Flynn and Will came up behind him, totally letting him take the lead. When they opened the doors and went in, it was definitely much colder.

"Wow." Flynn shivered, giving him a wide-eyed look.

"Yeah."

The automatic word generator attached to the EVP recorder blipped. "Bullet."

Blaine nodded. "That's right. You were shot here."

"Fuck. Amazing." Flynn sounded like his mind was blown.

"Uh-huh." Will had seen this kind of thing before, but he was clearly on board with this being an extremely good run.

A stroke brushed his wrist, and he made a show of jerking, spinning around, even though the touch wasn't harsh at all.

"What? What?" Flynn looked ecstatic, eyes wide, focused on Blaine.

"Something touched me! On the wrist!" *Sorry, honey. It's on camera. Are you okay?*

The touch came again, soft, gentle, like someone—she—was checking his pulse.

"Is it a good spirit or a bad one?" Flynn asked.

"Were you a nurse here? Are you Maryann? Maybe Donna Lewis? Or Renee?"

At the name Renee, the touch came again. "Renee? Hey. Hey, do you want to talk to us?"

"I can help you. What brings you here today?" Renee asked, voice warm, professionally concerned.

"Oh my God." Flynn's excited whisper seemed to echo all around the place.

Okay. Weird. Blaine was going to just go with it, though. "You did. We were worried about you."

"Worried about me? Honey, you're the one in the hospital." She took his wrist again, and it was a cold touch, but not in any way malevolent.

"I am." Oh fuck. He was going to pass out. "I totally…."

Flynn touched his shoulder, hand fucking warm, almost hot, compared to the specter's.

His knees buckled, and everything disappeared for a second, a dull thud at the base of his skull whispering, *"Room 204. Room 204. Room 204."*

Flynn caught him. He must have because when Blaine came back to himself, he was being held in Flynn's arms, and they were outside the ER, a few feet from the door. Will was speaking into his walkie-talkie, voice low and urgent.

"Blaine? Blaine, are you back with us?" Flynn asked.

"Yeah. Yeah, sorry." His head was pounding, and he felt like an elephant was sitting on his chest. The only solid thing that didn't hurt was where Flynn cradled him. His skin tingled like something important was going on all along where they touched.

"Blaine?" Will asked as Jason and Darnell came flying down the hall.

"Sorry. Sorry. Tell me we got that." She had been there. Right there.

"I got you fainting when Flynn touched you, yeah. And you were talking pretty good with someone. I heard it, but we'll have to see what the camera picked up."

Flynn nodded, hands rubbing up and down along Blaine's arms, warming him, spreading the tingles. "I totally heard her—she was trying to help you. One of the nurses, eh?"

"Renee. It was Renee. She spoke to me, guys, clear as a bell."

They all started talking at once.

"What did she say?"

"Tell me we got it on camera."

"No fucking way!"

"I heard it too, not that clear, but I heard it."

He let the clamor fade into the background, his brain running around in circles. He'd heard things before, sure. Felt things too, but nothing like this.

Flynn was still holding him, and he had to admit, it felt good, like he was keeping it together because of the tingly touches that Flynn shared with him. Crazy.

"Maybe we should pack it up for tonight, guys. Blaine's the color of milk." Darnell sounded worried as hell.

"Yeah, good idea," Jason said. "I vote we go back to Blaine's place. We can check out what we have that way. Save a few bucks on the motel too. The drive out here isn't that bad."

"Works for me. I got chips and Cokes and stuff." Blaine just wanted to go home and crawl in bed and… hell, he didn't know.

The guys came over and helped him and Flynn stand, and it was a physical wrench to not have Flynn's warmth supporting him anymore. Almost a pain inside him.

"You okay?" Flynn looked concerned and touched his arm.

The pain faded immediately.

"Fine. Totally. Just… that was intense."

Flynn nodded. "Yeah, my heart was in my throat until you opened your eyes again."

They got him turned around and headed to base camp at the other end of the hospital.

"Is it always like this?" Flynn asked.

"Shit, no," Darnell told him. "We haven't had this much excitement in ages. I mean, sometimes we get a good hit, but it's less often than we'd like."

"You must be a good-luck charm," Will said.

"Beginner's luck?" Flynn suggested. "I haven't had to sit through all the times when nothing happened. Yet."

They got back to base camp, and Jason and Darnell helped Will pack up most of their gear to take with them. It was too expensive to leave out in the open.

"How can I help?" Flynn asked.

"Get Blaine to the van, and get some water and a granola bar down his throat," Darnell suggested, coming up with one of each and handing them to Flynn.

Will tossed the keys at Flynn, who caught them, then touched Blaine's arm again. "Come on. We get to sit for a bit."

"I'm sorry. This doesn't happen very often." Honestly.

"Are you kidding? This was exciting. I mean, I'm sorry it seems to have knocked you for a loop, but you spoke with someone! Had an actual conversation. That is so cool." Flynn walked him to the van and opened the side door, encouraging him up into a seat. "I shouldn't have touched you, I guess, but you looked so pale."

He got seated, and Flynn joined him, then closed the door behind them to keep the bugs out. Flynn was about the only warm thing in the van, and Blaine had to admit he was happy they were sitting close enough that he could feel Flynn's warmth.

Flynn opened the bottle of water and handed it to him.

"Thanks." He sucked the water down, moaning happily.

Flynn opened the granola bar and handed it over when he was done with the water. "You're looking better already. You really had gone as white as a... well, ghost."

"It was a weird experience." And somehow it had been weirder with Flynn there.

"You wanna talk about it?" Flynn asked, settling in next to him and patting his thigh.

"She was superpresent. Usually I get whispers, feelings, not 'Hi, how are you?' You know?"

"How cool is that? You think it's because you've been here a lot and she knows you now? Recognizes you?"

"I don't know. Seriously. Did you see her? Hear her?"

"I didn't see anything, not really, but I could tell she was there, and I heard her. Not as clearly as you seem to have, but I could so tell you were having a conversation." Flynn's face was lit up, his excitement clear. "She was really there."

"Hopefully we got something on film." Blaine closed his eyes, his head pounding, throbbing. The anger had dissipated, though, which was good, because he didn't need that shit.

"You need anything?" Flynn asked, that hand coming back to rub Blaine's thigh. It was like Flynn couldn't stop touching him.

"Just to go home. I'm tired, and I have to be at work at 5:00 a.m....."

"Oh man. That's damn early. I'm sure the guys'll be here soon. You could nap on the drive home."

"Yeah. Saturdays are harsh, but it's worth it."

"Yeah? I'm glad because that was amazing. You're amazing." Flynn's eyes shone.

"I'm just...." He didn't know what he was. He felt drained, bone-deep.

Flynn suddenly wrapped his arms around Blaine and hugged him tight.

Invisible sparks flew between them, little explosions that faded slowly, leaving him... more peaceful?

"Sorry," murmured Flynn, sitting back. "You looked like you really needed that."

"No apologies." He had. He'd needed whatever that was.

"Cool." Flynn gave him another quick hug, then sat back and fished a small box of mints out of his pocket. He opened the container and offered Blaine the tiniest mints he'd ever seen. "They're cinnamon flavored."

"Those look like dollhouse candies."

Flynn chuckled. "They're small but mighty mints. They're good." Flynn passed the tin beneath his nose, the scent of cinnamon strong.

"Oh. Oh, that's cool. How many do I take?"

"As many as you want, man, but I find one at a time is more than enough cinnamon in my mouth. Your mileage might totally vary." Flynn's friendly dorkiness was a balm to the weirdness left over from his experience in the ER.

"Thanks." He took two and popped one in his mouth, the zing exactly what he was looking for.

Flynn put one in his own mouth and sprawled there next to him. There was a companionable silence between them that boded well for them being roommates.

Blaine let his eyes drop closed and focused on his breath. On his heartbeat.

It wasn't long before the guys arrived with the equipment, and suddenly the van was full of noise and busyness and they were on their way, bumping along the trail, headed home.

They were ramped up, chattering and bouncing, excited, but Blaine ignored it.

He needed to rest.

Chapter Four

FLYNN didn't have a whole lot to move, so it was probably just as well he was rooming with Blaine. If he'd gotten a place of his own, he'd have been swimming in it, using boxes as tables and sleeping on the floor. So it didn't take him long to move his stuff into Blaine's furnished spare room.

He spent a few minutes downing a bottle of water and giving the place a quick search to see where everything was.

The place was crazy—obviously handmade, but well-made. The kitchen was vast, with crazy mismatched granite counters and gorgeous handmade cabinets and tile floors that were obviously whatever Blaine had found. The island stood like a behemoth in the center of the room, the whole thing covered in groceries and stacks of mail.

The guys were crashed out in the huge open room that served as living/working/entertainment/dining area. There were two—*two*—sectionals, along with four recliners and a huge old farm table that creaked under the weight of their equipment.

A small bathroom downstairs served guests, and the upstairs had two more—one in Blaine's suite and one in his.

A suite.

He had a fucking suite. His rooms were more of the same—crazy tiles and finishings, but a huge comfortable bed and crazy dressers. A sitting area with a love seat and a rocker. Bookshelves.

It was horrifying and magical all at once. He was in love.

He thought maybe this was what Blaine's mind was like, this wonderful mishmash of stuff that shouldn't work together but totally did.

Flynn spent ten minutes putting away the groceries and another five sorting the mail into junk, bills, and miscellaneous. Then he grabbed a couple of bottles of water and headed down to the farm stand. Although really, stand was a bit of a misnomer. The place was almost a store, all kinds of produce and homemade jams, jellies, canned vegetables.

Blaine had to be exhausted. He was drenched with sweat and had dark circles under his eyes. "Hey. You get some sleep?"

"Yeah, I did. And now I'm all moved in." Flynn handed over the water. "Why don't you go take a nap? I can handle this for a while." He was sure he could figure things out. He was a smart guy.

"It's cool. Mom and Dad would freak out. They haven't even met you yet. Have a seat, if you want."

"The least I can do is keep you company. You guys can't hire someone to help out on the busy days?" Flynn figured the weekend had to be huge for the market, but that was the same time as they did their ghost hunting. It didn't seem fair Blaine was the one holding the bag all the time.

"We could, but... they do lots for me, and there's the cancer, you know? It's okay. I don't mind. It's only the summers that are killer busy. It's starting to wind down. We'll have a little boost at Christmas, but that's it."

"What about the jams and canning the vegetables and stuff—who does all that?" Because that seemed like an even harder job than running the store to Flynn. He might like to eat food, but he wasn't into preparing it. Especially for storage like that.

"My mom, my aunt Patty, my aunt Yolanda. They have a little cottage industry."

"I bet it's good stuff." He browsed through the goods, finding the jars full of preserved fruit and vegetables fascinating. Almost like ghost veggies and fruits, locked forever at the moment of their death. He shook himself. God, he was a nutjob sometimes.

A short caravan of cars pulled up, people buying apples and pumpkins, butternut squash, and corn and walnuts. It was a crazy flurry of business, and then they were alone again.

It kind of left him blinking, and he chuckled. "That was something." He didn't quite know what, but it was definitely something.

"Yeah, I know." Blaine grinned at him, and it hit him how lovely Blaine was, long-haired and loose-limbed with big bright eyes. "They're like birds."

"I do love the way you see the world." Blaine was like a free spirit, only he was grounded at the same time. Flynn found himself moving closer.

"You want a drink, man?"

"I've got my water." He hefted it to show Blaine. "But thanks." He stopped short of actually rubbing shoulders with Blaine, but it was a near thing. Now that he was letting himself look without anything else— like ghosts—coloring his perception, he found himself definitely attracted. Oh, he had been from the start, but it was deeper now. Sexier.

"We make one hell of a cup of coffee, and the chai is stunning. Mom will start with hot apple cider next weekend."

"Oh well, in that case. Let me try the chai." He wasn't really much of a tea drinker, but if Blaine thought it was stunning, he wanted to try it.

"Sure." The chai was in a little heated container, and the liquid that came out of the spout was fragrant, milky, and wonderful.

Flynn took the cup and buried his nose in the steam. "Mmm. It definitely smells good." He took a careful sip, finding that the flavor danced on his tongue. "Oh, it *is* stunning."

"Thanks! My recipe." Blaine took a goofy little bow.

Flynn laughed softly, utterly charmed by this man. "You invent other foodstuffs?" Maybe Blaine should have a cookbook out here along with the canned goods.

"I like to cook. I like mixing flavors up."

"You ever thought of doing a cookbook? You've got perfect product placement if you're selling stuff that you use in the recipes." He took another sip of the chai, liking the way it warmed him up. Not that he was cold—he was very warm-blooded—but still, it was a pleasant sensation.

"We've done one with community farm-to-table recipes. Just a silly self-published thing."

"That's great! That's what I'm talking about. Did it sell well?" He looked around, not seeing any copies. Was that a good sign?

"Okay, yeah. We'll bring it back out for Christmas shoppers."

"That's great—you're a published author. I'm jealous." He smiled at Blaine, happy for him. Somehow, being accomplished in a hodgepodge of different things seemed right for Blaine. Suited him. He tried to imagine the man in a suit and just couldn't.

"I'm a dude who makes great chai and sees ghosts."

"See? Totally jealous here." He'd love to actually see his mom, not just feel her presence. It wasn't a mean kind of jealousy or anything. Maybe envy would be a better word. Oh yeah, he really was a dork, and he was glad he hadn't said any of that out loud.

"Dude, you're a scientist with a degree. My folks are going to think you're the best thing ever."

"Yeah? Is that what parents like? Degrees? Not happy kids who are pursuing their dreams?" He thought Blaine was brave.

"Shit. Happy kids who are pursuing their dreams is code for shiftless loser son who can't commit."

Flynn found himself needing to comfort Blaine, so he reached out and touched his shoulder. "You don't believe that describes you, do you?"

Blaine shrugged. "They never say that, but I know."

"Ah, man." Like he had the night before, he pulled Blaine into a hug, feeling like Blaine really needed it.

Blaine was stiff for a heartbeat; then he relaxed, melted into the touch. They stayed like that for a few minutes, simply hugging. Flynn didn't get a whole lot of hugs in his life, and he was enjoying the contact, the human part of this whole making-friends thing.

A car pulled up, reminding him where they were, and he reluctantly let go, stepped back. He offered Blaine a warm smile, though.

"Time to work, buddy," Blaine said. "Have your chai."

"Thanks, man. You don't mind if I sit in the corner here and hang out?"

"Of course not. We close in half an hour, and we're closed Sunday through Wednesday, this time of year."

"Cool. So we can hang out then, get to know each other better." Because Flynn wanted to. He wanted to learn all about Blaine.

"I'd like that. After I get to sleep in on Sunday, right?"

"You'll need that if we're going back out to the hospital tonight. And I promise I won't wake you so we can talk." He was a considerate roommate.

"Yeah, weekends are always tough, but worth it."

"Good, good. It'd suck if you didn't think so." Flynn knew what it was to have a lot on your plate. He'd been doing school and working odd jobs on weekends and during the summer for a while. He'd received a substantial settlement after the wreck that killed his parents, which his aunt had put aside until he'd turned eighteen, but working meant it had stretched past university so that now he could afford to be without pay—for a while at least.

He watched Blaine interact with the customers, loving how easy the man was, how sincere and gentle. Everything Flynn had learned about the guy told him he was an all-around good guy. It was great to see.

As soon as the latest group of people left, Blaine started packaging up food, putting different things different places.

Flynn finished up his chai and tossed the container in the bin. "You sure I can't help with anything?"

"Do you want to help me put together the food-bank boxes? The food that needs eating before Thursday will go in, and Dad will deliver half to people close by, and the other half I'll run to the food bank Monday."

"Cool, I'd love to help out. Just let me know what needs to go where."

"Grab those plastic bins from the back, huh?"

Flynn headed back and found a good-sized storage room filled with bins and books, a chair, coffee and snacks, and random decorations.

The space suited Blaine to a *T*. Grinning, Flynn grabbed the plastic bins and went back to Blaine, who was sorting and whistling, a half-eaten apple beside him.

He loved how easygoing Blaine was, how he simply got to work and didn't seem to stress over it.

Flynn put the bins in a row on the ground.

"So," Blaine explained, "you put six apples in each, and then all the rest of the summer veg that's still out— the tomatoes, the okra. I think there's a watermelon or two left."

"Cool. It's great that this stuff doesn't go to waste." Flynn started filling the boxes as directed.

"Dad has always been into supporting the community that supports us, you know?"

"It's a great philosophy."

"I think so, yeah. Some of the older folks are in real need of good, solid food."

Flynn nodded and hummed as he continued to divide the food among the boxes.

They were interrupted by the sound of whistling as an older man who looked an awful lot like Blaine came in.

"Dad! Hey!"

"Hey, son. Who's this? A new friend? Another ghostbuster?"

"Yep. And a new roommate. Flynn, my dad, John. Dad, Flynn, tech guy."

Flynn wiped his hands on his jeans and held one out. "Nice to meet you, sir."

"Pleased. Tech guy, huh? You do websites and stuff?"

"That and also run the stats, come up with programs to work with the ghost-capturing hardware, run analysis, that kind of thing." And spend nights in dark scary places looking for specters. Wasn't that what every nerd did?

"Huh. That's cool. You in school?"

"Just graduated, sir. And I got my dream job." There weren't a lot of ghost-hunting jobs out there.

"Excellent. Well, I know that you guys are busy tonight, so Mom says everyone come to the house for supper. She's got stew and cornbread."

"Oh wow, that sounds delicious. Thank you, sir." He shook John's hand again, thinking it was a good sign that Blaine's mother was up to cooking. She must be doing okay.

John grunted, then looked at his son, shook his head. "I'll finish up here, boy. You look exhausted. Catch a nap."

"I'm okay."

"Do as you're told."

Now there was a dad voice, even if Flynn had never had one aimed at him before. He ducked his head, staying out of it, and made for the exit in case Blaine and his father needed to talk.

"Thanks, Pop. The cash box is locked up in the safe already."

John's answer faded as Flynn stepped out of the store area. He sat on a picnic bench, waiting for Blaine to join him.

Blaine came out, a huge box of vegetables and fruit in his arms. "Pop says this is for us."

"Cool, that's really nice of him. Our grocery bill should be smaller this week, shouldn't it?" He went and took the box from Blaine. "I got it. You've been working all day." Besides, it was just one more box to carry in.

"Yeah? Thanks. I'm…. Are the guys grilling? Tell me they aren't just setting random fires…."

Flynn sniffed. "Grilling, I think. It smells good anyway. They were still asleep when I came out. We'd better tell them we're invited to your folks' for dinner."

"Totally. I'm going to jump in the shower and catch a twenty-minute nap."

"Sure. I'll let the guys know about the invite. It was okay that I said yes, right?" He didn't think John was just being polite, but he could have misread the signs. He didn't always pick up on social cues the best.

"Totally. They bitch, but they like you guys."

"Okay. I just wanted to make sure." He bumped hips with Blaine. "You go get your shower. I'll deal with the guys' fire-making and put away this stuff. What time do we need to be ready to go over?"

"We'll eat at five and head out to the hospital again at six thirty."

"Works for me. Have a good nap." He followed Blaine in and headed for the kitchen to drop the box there before going out to talk to the guys. So far this new endeavor was working out great.

Chapter Five

"**GODDAMN** it!" Blaine slammed out of the hospital, livid.

Seriously? All that activity yesterday and nothing tonight? Not a fucking blip?

"Hey, it happens, right?" Flynn said, following him with the laptop and the EMF reader. "We have to keep trying."

"Yeah. Yeah, whatever. It was just… yesterday…."

Yesterday had rocked.

"Yeah, it was a great first time. I'm glad it was yesterday that was good. If it had been like today, I would have been really discouraged."

"Most nights are like tonight," Darnell said, carrying equipment past them to the van.

"A lot of nights, but not most," Jason countered. "It's a fine line, but it is a line."

"It's disappointing, though."

You should have taken them to 204.

"Yeah." Flynn bobbed his head in agreement. "But we'll look at the data and see if we can't figure out why yesterday was so much better. I mean, maybe something as simple as the weather can make a difference."

God, the man was a Pollyanna. Which wasn't a bad thing, but aggravating when he wanted to wallow in his annoyance for a while.

Blaine really wanted to burst into tears and take a nap.

They packed up the van and all climbed in, Flynn settling in beside him.

"Fifty percent hit rate's pretty good, isn't it?"

"Yeah. Yeah, it was just so big before, you know?" And he was so tired.

"Yeah. Weird that it wouldn't be good again tonight. But maybe the ghosts were tired. Oh! Maybe it was because you're tired, so you didn't feel it because your energy is low. Maybe that's why they weren't drawn to you this time." Flynn shook his head. "I'm babbling."

"Babble away." Blaine could sleep through anything. Anything.

"I'll be good. Try and process internally for a while." Flynn gave him a wry smile.

Jason plopped down on the other side of him, Darnell sitting up front with Will again. Then they were off, bumping along the road.

Gently knocking his shoulder, Jason leaned in. "You okay, man?"

"I am. Disappointed. Tired. But okay."

Jason sighed and nodded. "Yeah. I think this might have been the least successful night we've had at the hospital. I think we should do it again next weekend. Maybe we'll get lucky again."

"Maybe." Maybe he'd go out on his own tomorrow night, if only to see if he was losing his mind.

"We could always go out tomorrow night," Jason suggested, as if reading Blaine's thoughts. "I know we don't usually work Sunday nights because Darnell has a day job, but we could make an exception."

"What about during the day?" Flynn asked from his other side. "Do you guys do any hunting during daylight hours?"

"We could do that. Hell, it's supposed to be cold and clammy tomorrow," Darnell pointed out. "Overcast. Could be cool. I'm in."

Flynn and Jason both looked at Blaine expectantly. They usually didn't do days because one or more of them tended to be working, and when they went out Friday and Saturday nights, they usually slept the weekend days away. They'd ended early tonight, though, given the poor luck they'd had, and they could still sleep in and spend the afternoon back at the hospital.

He nodded, both Jason and Darnell whooping like they'd won a prize. Flynn smiled at him, eyes full of life.

"You guys can stay at the barn if you want. But I'm going to crash."

"Be a quicker turnaround this evening if we do," Will noted.

Darnell and Jason both nodded their agreement.

"It'll be my first official night in my new home," Flynn noted. "Thanks again for having me."

"You're welcome. You'll work out just fine." At least he hoped so.

"I'll do my best. I'll try not to be all about the shoptalk too. It'd be a bit much if we were on it twenty-four seven. At least I think it would."

"Uh-huh." He dozed a little, the sound of David's voice such a comfort. Wait. *David?*

Everything faded, and Blaine wasn't hearing words anymore, only the sound washing over him, letting him sleep.

"Hey, man, we're home."

"Good deal." He opened his eyes, surprised for a second to see the barn, which was stupid because he'd lived at the farm his entire life, and he'd lived in the barn for five years.

"You were out pretty good," Flynn told him. "Fast asleep. It was almost a shame to wake you. You can have something to eat now, though, before bed." Flynn climbed out of the van and smiled back at him.

"Uh-huh." He got out too. "Are we leaving the shit in the van?"

"Yeah. It's safe in there."

They all made their way into the barn, and Flynn headed right for the kitchen. "Grilled cheese sandwiches sound good?"

"Yeah. Great." Those were perfect two-in-the-morning snacks.

Blaine sat at the big table with the guys, listening to the chatter as they talked about what a bust tonight had been but how they were all hopeful for tomorrow.

When the sandwiches were handed out, they weren't pretty, but they smelled good, and his stomach rumbled. Flynn grinned as he took the seat next to Blaine's.

"Thanks, man." Blaine ate half of one, his entire body heavy.

Flynn put an arm around his shoulders, and it felt good. "You okay, Blaine? Just tired?"

"Yeah. Yeah, it's tough, Saturday night." He ran on too little sleep and too much adrenaline.

"How about we get you to bed, then?" Flynn stood and helped him up, hand at his elbow, steadying him when he swayed. "Oh man. You're worn out."

"I am." *Come sleep with me.*

"I wish there was a way we could help you out so you could get some sleep during the day too. It would make your Saturday nights easier."

Blaine couldn't remember the last time someone had looked out for him, worried over whether he got enough sleep. Aside from his parents of course.

"I'm okay." They headed upstairs, and Flynn came right into his bedroom with him, like it was the most natural thing ever.

Flynn tugged off his sweater, then pushed him down onto his bed and bent to take off his sneakers.

He blinked like a moron, watching Flynn.

Flynn untied and slipped off his right sneaker, then his left. His socks were next, Flynn balling them together before tossing them along the floor.

"You'll be more comfortable if you at least get the jeans off."

"Uh-huh." He just about managed to get his belt unbuckled.

Flynn shook his head and made a soft noise. "I'm not coming on to you, okay? Just helping out." Flynn undid the top button and carefully pulled down the zipper. "I want you to be awake when I come on to you."

"You want to come on to me?" No one had in so long.

Color lit up Flynn's cheeks, and he ducked his head a moment before meeting Blaine's eyes again and smiling. "Yeah. I kinda do. Where kinda means really."

"Oh. Good to know."

Flynn tugged Blaine's pants and underwear off, then pushed him back gently, and he found himself on his back, looking up at the ceiling.

"Stay and talk for a second?" he asked.

"Sure." Flynn grabbed Blaine's feet and put them on the bed before flipping the edge of the comforter over him. "Is it okay if I lie on the bed?"

"Uh-huh. Please." He wanted some company.

Flynn climbed up and lay on his side next to Blaine, then gave him a smile. "You got anything in particular you want to talk about or just shoot the breeze?"

"Tell me about yourself." *Talk to me.*

Flynn chuckled. "Yeah, really? Like, I was born in Montreal. My favorite food is poutine. That kind of thing?"

At his lazy nod, Flynn went on. "Okay. I guess I can do that. My folks died when I was five. A car accident. They were hit by a drunk driver at three in the afternoon. That's the part that still gets me. It was the middle of the day."

"I'm sorry, honey." That sucked.

"It was a long time ago. And like I said the other day, my mom never really left me. She's always been there when I needed her. I had an aunt who lived in a little town outside of Ottawa who took me in. She wasn't terribly warm, but she didn't abuse me or anything, and I had everything I needed. Not everything I wanted, but everything I needed." Flynn laughed softly. "So I would say I'm not at all spoiled."

"I probably am." Blaine didn't know, really. He hadn't had everything, but he had plenty. He had family and food and shelter and random fun.

"Nah—you work too hard to be spoiled. And then there's the giving food to those in need thing. You're safe."

"Oh good." He let his eyelids close. "So why science?"

"Because for as long as I can remember, I've asked why. About everything. Why things work the way they do, etc. And then there's my mom. I learned pretty quickly that my belief in her still being with me was not shared. Like at all. And I wanted to prove that it's true. That it's not my imagination."

"No. It's not." It might be all his imagination—Blaine wasn't sure. Or his own insanity.

Flynn nodded. "Yeah. Yeah, it's not. Anyway. So that's why science. My innate curiosity. You know, I can probably thank Aunt Judy for that—every time I asked why, she'd tell me to go look it up. So I'd write it down, and when we went to the library, which we did once a week, I'd look up everything on my list."

"Cool." He could imagine that—little David with his schoolbooks and his glasses, looking through books.

"I still love reference books. I might have several boxes worth in storage. Reference books, history books, science manuals. I've got fiction too. I love spy thrillers and sci-fi the best."

"I read." Blaine nodded. He loved horror and thrillers, romances, gothic stuff. He'd been going to school for English lit, after all.

Flynn laughed, the sound almost a giggle. "That almost sounds like 'Hey, I know how.' I know what you meant, though. A lot of people don't, though, after finishing high school." Flynn shrugged. "I like it. I find it relaxing, informative. It was always a refuge growing up too. Aunt Judy couldn't afford hockey equipment, so I didn't play in any youth leagues. Just on the street with the other kids in the neighborhood."

"Not a sport guy. Not my thing."

"I like staying in shape, and I prefer running around chasing a ball to do it. I do street hockey and pickup soccer games. Nothing organized." Flynn touched Blaine's belly, rubbed it. "How do you stay so skinny?"

"I work hard, mostly. My life's pretty active." Farm life tended to be.

"Have you got a farmer's tan?" Flynn asked, grinning.

"Do I?"

Flynn pushed up the arm of his T-shirt and hooted. "You do! Although, it's not like you're super pale. You must work with your shirt off some of the time so that your arms are darker than the rest of you, but you're still tanned all over. Unless your belly isn't tanned...."

It was a leading comment. Even exhausted, Blaine could tell that.

He yanked up his T-shirt, knowing his belly was pretty damn tan. He was a bit of a sun-worshiper.

"Damn...." Flynn reached out and stroked his abs, the touch gentle but sending tingles through Blaine for all its softness. "So pretty."

"Oh...." The sensation made his toes curl.

"You feel that too? I've never felt anything like when I touch your skin." Flynn kept going, tracing Blaine's abs, eyes following his fingers as they moved on Blaine's skin.

"Uh-huh. This is a bad idea—hooking up with your new roommate." He didn't want it to stop.

"I know. And you're tired, and I said I wouldn't come on to you right now." Flynn didn't stop touching him, and it was getting better, the sensation seeming to build on itself.

"Uh-huh." He drew Flynn deeper into the bed.

"Of course if you're coming on to me, then I suppose it doe—"

He cut Flynn off with a kiss, pressing their lips together. The words buzzed between them for a moment; then Flynn moaned and melted into the kiss, opening his mouth.

Blaine sighed happily, floating with the soft buzz they were building. He had to admit, there was more to this than any other first kiss he'd shared. That strange, but good, tingle that came whenever they touched was there in spades, adding to his enjoyment of the kiss. Maybe it was some weird body-chemistry thing. He didn't care.

Flynn rested along his side, continuing to stroke his belly as their tongues slid together. He was trying to focus, to stay awake, because he didn't want to miss a second of this.

Humming, Flynn settled his whole hand on Blaine's belly, rubbing now instead of randomly tracing. This touch was firmer, and he felt it all the way to his toes.

How did Flynn know how he liked it? How did Flynn know what he needed?

Their tongues tangled some more. Flynn smiled, moving their lips apart, then together again, and he pushed slightly closer, making Blaine more aware of his lack of clothing next to Flynn's completely dressed state. Regardless of the material between them, he could feel the heat from Flynn's cock, the flesh hard.

"You want me." His own cock was filling, telling him he wasn't really *that* tired.

Flynn met his gaze and nodded. "I do. You're a gorgeous, sexy man, and we have chemistry together."

"Uh-huh." They sure had a spark; that was evident.

"You want me to go, just say so. I know you're tired." Flynn's words might have been saying that, but his eyes were telling an entirely different story. One that said "I want to stay."

"Stay?" That was what they both wanted, after all.

"Yes, please." Flynn nodded, then brought their lips back together for more of the slow, easy kisses that Blaine could feel all through himself.

Flynn toed his shoes off, and then they were snuggling, tongues sliding against each other as they twisted their legs together.

After pushing up beneath Blaine's T-shirt, Flynn slid his hand from Blaine's belly to his nipples and stroked them gently.

Blaine's breath huffed out, the light tingles making his eyes cross.

"Sensitive?" Flynn asked, looking pleased about that and stroking them again.

"Feels good. Erotic. Hot."

"I like that. Can we take your T-shirt off?" Flynn tugged at it, and Blaine shifted, leaning up and raising his arms so Flynn could pull it over his head.

Groaning, Flynn leaned in and touched his tongue to the tip of Blaine's left nipple. The caress was achingly sweet, and he moaned with the rush of pure, easy pleasure. He felt Flynn's smile against his skin before the touch came again, Flynn's tongue hotter this time, pressing a little harder against the nub of flesh.

Blaine wiggled slowly, feeling like he was sinking under water. Flynn hummed, and the sound vibrated along Blaine's nipple and into his chest. Then Flynn sucked for a moment before moving to lick at Blaine's collarbone and the hollow of his neck. Next Flynn kissed his Adam's apple and under his chin. Each touch spoke of care and brought shivers of pleasure with it.

"Kiss me again, babe." He wanted to taste.

Flynn didn't have to be asked twice, pressing their lips together again in a kiss that was less careful and soft than their first ones had been. As they kissed, Flynn drew his hands all over Blaine's chest, tracing his abs, then his nipples, then sliding down along his breastbone right to his navel.

Blaine found Flynn's ass with his hands and squeezed tight, rocking them together, nice and easy. Flynn moaned for him, the sound tasting good in his mouth.

There were still too many clothes between them, but he was feeling so good right where they were and with what they were doing that he hated to stop to remove them.

And it felt wicked, naughty, to have Flynn still in his jeans while he was bare. Flynn shifted so he was mostly on top of Blaine, rocking slowly, dragging the denim along his cock and his belly.

"Damn. Damn, man." He wrapped one arm around Flynn's shoulders. Were they really doing this?

"This okay?" Flynn asked, staring down at him, body stilling.

"Uh-huh. More than. More than." It felt necessary.

"Thank God." Flynn kissed him again and rocked their bodies together, the denim of his jeans scraping along Blaine's skin. It wasn't gentle, but it didn't hurt.

Blaine worked Flynn's shirt from under his waistband, finding skin. It was warm and smooth against his fingers, and his touch made Flynn moan, buck against him. He searched for scars, for marks, his fingers insisting there should be some. There wasn't a single one, though, Flynn's skin smooth and warm, with just a little fur on his pecs and a thin treasure trail on his belly. Flynn pushed happily into his caresses.

"God, I have to get these jeans off." Despite the muttered words, Flynn kept on rocking against him.

"Uh-huh. Come on. Gimme."

Flynn chuckled, not stilling, not shifting, not trying to get at his jeans one-handed or anything. Just the maddening gentle rolling together of their bodies. "Gimme?"

"You. I want you. Bad." That was as coherent as Blaine got.

"Oh." Flynn giggled and stopped rocking, holding himself up with one arm as he tried to open up his jeans one-handed. "A little help would make this go faster."

"Right. Right. Helping hands make light work." The little children's rhyme made him chuckle.

Flynn chuckled too and sucked in his belly, giving Blaine room to work open the top button of Flynn's jeans.

"Like how you smell." That was so important, especially when blow jobs were involved.

"Yeah? Soap and water." Flynn's eyes lit up with his smile. "I like the way you taste."

"Sweat and hard work?" he teased.

"Yeah, maybe. Whatever it is, I like it." Flynn kissed him again, tongue sweeping through his mouth, making it hard to concentrate on pulling down Flynn's zipper.

He traced his fingertips along Flynn's swollen mushroom head through his briefs, the barest touch.

Flynn's eyes went wide, and he gasped softly. "Oh damn. Blaine."

"Yeah. You're hot as hell."

"You too. Sexy. Uh…."

It looked like Blaine's touches were making Flynn incoherent. Score.

Flynn pushed at his jeans and underwear, rubbing up and bumping against Blaine as he tried to kick them off.

Blaine found himself getting tickled, and he kept touching, teasing, and playing.

"Not helping!" There was no real heat in the words; a hint of laughter threaded through them.

"No?" Blaine leaned up and took another kiss, the connection sharp and happy.

Flynn moaned into the kiss and before their lips parted again, finally got his jeans and underwear off, and they were both naked.

Damn, that was fine. Blaine hadn't had the luxury of skin in so long that he'd forgotten the wonderful shock of it. Flynn rocked against him once more, giving him lots of skin-on-skin action.

"Oh God, you feel good."

"Uh-huh. You do. I do. Don't stop, okay?"

"Got it. No stopping." Flynn grinned suddenly, eyes twinkling like crazy. "Not even if you fall asleep on me."

"Yeah, yeah. Seducing the snoozing man. You have to watch that."

Flynn shook his head. "No, I said I wasn't going to do that—I'm pretty sure you seduced me."

"Did I? Not bad for someone who's exhausted, huh?"

"Not bad at all. I can't wait to see what happens when you're fully awake." Flynn continued sliding their bodies together.

"I'm a sex god. Just you wait." Blaine cracked himself up.

Flynn laughed with him, face happy and bright. Then he gasped as their cocks bumped hard.

There was nothing funny about that at all.

Groaning, Flynn brought their mouths back together again, continuing the long, sliding motion that pushed their cocks together.

Blaine reached between them and found their pricks, wrapped his fingers around them, and began to stroke, nice and slow, up and down.

"Oh God, yes. Your hand feels so good. So good." Flynn's eyes closed, his face a study in pleasure.

All Blaine could do was nod and keep stroking. That was his best.

They moved together easily, sensations building one on top of the other until they were panting and speeding up, orgasms growing closer.

Blaine took a sloppy kiss, his body barely following his brain's instructions. Flynn was rolling against him hard, though, keeping them moving, the pleasure flowing between them. It felt so large, so odd and wonderful, so right.

"Blaine. Oh God." Flynn stared at him, gaze intense.

"Uh-huh. Gonna. Ready?"

"God yes." Flynn nodded and added his hand to Blaine's on their cocks.

The extra pressure was all Blaine needed, all he wanted, all he could bear. He came, heat spraying between them. Then there was more, Flynn's moan filling his room.

Oh hell yeah.

Blaine slumped, his whole body going boneless.

"Oh God, that was good. It was really good." Flynn collapsed half-on him, half-off. He pressed kisses against Blaine's neck and cheek.

He'd missed this kind of intimacy. So much. Sweet man. "Thank you."

"And thank you. Is it okay if I rest with you awhile?"

"Uh-huh." Of course. Of course it was okay. Silly man.

"Cool." Flynn looked around, eyes at half-mast and sleepy looking. Then he reached over and grabbed a few Kleenex from the bedside table and cleaned them up before dropping next to Blaine. On his side, Flynn cuddled in.

"Sleep well, honey. So glad we're home."

"Sure thing, Blaine." Flynn kissed his cheek, eyes dropping closed all the way as Flynn let out a long, soft sigh.

Blaine moaned, sinking into dreams of white sheets and bright lights and David's sweet voice.

Chapter Six

FLYNN was glad they'd come back to the hospital. Sure last night had been disappointing, but their first night had been awesome. It was neat coming back during the day too. While it was still fairly dark in the hospital, it felt less spooky than it did at night. Of course for all he knew that was going to mean they wouldn't get any hits. He just didn't know, but it would be interesting to see.

"Are we going to check out upstairs today?" They hadn't ventured up there at all, barring the quick look he and Blaine had done on Friday.

"No." Blaine shook his head, refusing to meet his eyes. "Let's focus on the ER."

"Oh, okay." Flynn shrugged. He supposed that was where they'd gotten the great hit, but on Friday Blaine had been excited about the second floor, and that's where they'd set up the overnight cameras. Not that they'd caught anything. "You think Renee will come back today?"

"I hope so. Come on. Let's go explore. Cameras are ready?"

Will nodded. "They are."

"Let's do this thing." Darnell hoisted his camera too. Jason trailed them with a boom mike for better sound.

"Lead on," Flynn added, all smiles. He was trying not to bounce too much or get too excited in case it was another bust. But he was hopeful.

Blaine pushed his braid back behind his shoulder, smiling into the lens. "Hey, we're at the Eugene Thurston Memorial Hospital, and we're hoping to get some activity. We were here a couple of days ago, and we encountered an entity we believe to be a nurse who was gunned down here in the emergency room."

Flynn began using the EMF reader as they walked toward the ER, searching high and low for some hits.

"The entity made contact with me, asking me if I needed assistance and trying to take my pulse."

"We all felt the sudden cold when the entity showed up," Flynn added. Even if they hadn't gotten anything concrete on the damn cameras. Yeah, there had been something indistinct and some sounds, but nothing they could say was more than normal sounds of an abandoned building. Certainly nothing like the mumbling he'd heard, let alone the actual conversation Blaine had been having with her.

That, to him, was more frustrating than them not getting a single thing yesterday—the obvious hits they'd been getting on Friday night that they just couldn't prove.

Blaine closed his eyes, face turning toward the stairs, and Flynn swore Blaine shook his head like he was arguing.

"Is there something upstairs, Blaine?" Flynn headed toward him, the guys following.

"Just dust." That was a lie. He knew that.

What he didn't know was why Blaine didn't want to go up there. Maybe whatever Blaine was getting from up there was pretty fucking scary. He let it drop. If they didn't get a hit in the emergency room today, he could suggest they go upstairs instead.

They all followed Blaine down the main hall toward the ER. Flynn didn't know if it was his imagination or not, but he thought it was beginning to get cooler. Not cold, but… a temperature change.

Blaine walked, his eyes closed like last time, unerringly toward the area where the four nurses died. Flynn moved in closer than he'd been yesterday or Friday, feeling the need to protect Blaine.

Will stayed right on them, the camera like a growth from his face.

Flynn tried to ignore it, or at least be cool about it, but he wasn't nearly as sanguine about it as Blaine was, and he kept worrying whether he should be keeping the narration going or something when Blaine wasn't talking.

"I feel like things are heavy here, like there's a…." Blaine stopped, hand reaching out for a second.

Flynn held his breath and worked the EMF reader, trying to pick something up. He couldn't see anything, or hear it.

Suddenly the EMF went off, the lights glowing red. "We got a hit!"

He knew he was bouncing like a loon, but he was excited.

"Are you getting anything else, Blaine? Is she back?" Was he making it harder for Blaine by talking? He'd have to check some other time when they weren't filming and here in the middle of it all.

He wasn't sure Blaine even heard him. He wasn't sure Blaine even cared.

Flynn strained to see or hear something. Then he felt a touch, like a hand sliding down his back, and he gasped, shivered. "Something touched me."

He spun around, and for a second he swore Blaine was standing there, but that wasn't possible because Blaine was in front of him.

Flynn blinked and looked again. Whatever he'd seen was gone. "Shit, that was spooky." And weird. "What do you see?" he asked Blaine.

Blaine shook his head as if to clear it. "Did you guys hear that? 'Can you help us? We're here in the ER.'"

"Oh God. That's amazing. I didn't hear that, but I definitely felt something. Someone touched me on the back." He laughed softly. "I turned, and for a minute I thought it was you, which is crazy because you were in front of me the whole time."

"Yeah? Weird. Will? You see anything?"

"Shadows. And it's like fucking December in here."

"Didn't see anything," Jason noted. And Darnell agreed.

"So they want our help?" Flynn asked. "What can we do for them? Do they know they're dead?"

Blaine stood there, silent, still, weirdly unfocused.

Flynn glanced at the other guys. "Is this normal?" It wasn't like anything that had happened in the last couple of days, but maybe it did happen. He didn't know. It seemed off, though, kind of creepy and wrong.

"Blaine? Blaine, man, you okay?" Will frowned behind the camera. "Blaine!"

Okay, so not normal.

Flynn grabbed Blaine's arm and squeezed, and an electric jolt thrilled through him, almost like he'd touched a live wire. He gasped and squeezed tighter. "Blaine! Come on. Talk to me."

"Huh? I'm cool. I'm cool." Blaine shook his head, blinking for a moment.

"Your skin sure is." It was cold to the touch. Flynn rubbed his hands along Blaine's arms, trying to warm him up. "You have goose bumps."

Will walked up and pushed the camera into Blaine's face. "You okay, man?"

"Chilled."

Flynn snorted. "Yeah. To the bone by the looks of you. What's going on, Blaine? You've got to talk to us."

"I thought I…. I don't know. I feel a little heavy and totally chilled."

Flynn hugged Blaine, trying to impart body warmth but also worried. "We gotta get him warmed up, guys."

Darnell put down the boom and came around to hug Blaine from the back. Flynn nodded. Between the two of them, this should work, right? Unless of course the ghost was, like, inside Blaine or something.

"You know who you are, right?"

"Sure I do! I'm not crazy!"

"Hey, I never said that. I was just worried that…." Well, it sounded stupid now that he was about to say it out loud.

"What?" Will asked.

Flynn shrugged and let go of Blaine. "Possessed or something." Oh yeah, it definitely sounded stupid saying it out loud. But he was worried for Blaine—honestly worried. He didn't want anything to happen to the guy.

Darnell was the first one to start laughing, and then they were all cracking up, ending the tension.

He rolled his eyes at himself. "Sorry, man. Shit happened, and you got chilled from the sudden drop in temperature, and I guess I kind of freaked." It had been really weird, though. And he'd had the sense Blaine was being taken away from him, which was crazy.

"He's new," Will teased. "He worries."

"Like we all haven't had our moments, huh?" Blaine rubbed his arms, looking like the man Flynn knew—the one he'd rubbed off with a few hours ago.

"I'll try not to overreact again."

"Can we get back to filming already?" Jason asked.

Flynn nodded. "You want to tell us what you saw or felt, and then we'll go in?"

"It was cold, and I thought I heard someone crying, but I could have been wrong. It happens, you know?"

"Yeah. Are you okay now? Should we go on?" Flynn was totally willing to let Blaine take the lead here.

"Yeah. Yeah, of course. I'm golden."

Blaine wandered in and out of different empty, dusty bays, taking readings and muttering to himself.

Flynn shrugged and went with it. Who was he to say Blaine wasn't being on the up-and-up? He'd only just met the guy, and one shared orgasm didn't give him permission to make like he knew Blaine better than the rest of the guys.

He felt like he did, though, and the worry sat like a bird of prey on his shoulder.

Blaine looked weirdly haunted, a bit drawn, which was stupid, wasn't it?

Flynn kept his mouth shut but watched Blaine closely. If he thought something was taking Blaine over again like he had earlier, he was interfering.

He didn't like that thought, that his friend—lover—might get taken over.

The EMF reader started going crazy again. "Do you see anything, Blaine?"

"Look at all the pretty horses."

Who said that? Was that Blaine?

He looked over to Will, who had the camera glued to them.

"Blaine? Say again?"

"I didn't say anything."

"Yes, you did." That was Jase, over the earphones. "Something about horses."

"Yeah, Jase is right." Flynn nodded. He was sure they'd gotten that on camera this time. "Is someone here? Someone besides the five of us?"

"The meters are going wild, man." Darnell was a little wild-eyed.

"Uh-huh." Flynn nodded vigorously and nudged Blaine. He should have been excited too and narrating this. Something was wrong if he wasn't on it, Flynn was sure. "Blaine? Is there someone here?"

"Horses. You have to watch for the horses." Blaine blinked and then grinned, the look false, a sham. "Man, look at all the sensors. We must have lit the place up."

"You're fucking right we did," Darnell said. "But what's with the fucking horses?"

"Yeah." Will focused in on Blaine. "Tell us what the heck that was all about."

Flynn didn't say anything, but he wanted to know too.

"What horses?"

"Yeah, that's what we want to know." Flynn put his hand on Blaine's forehead. He was chilled again. "You keep telling us about the horses. To look at them and watch out for them. Have you ever had a ghost take you over before?" Because really, that was the only thing that made sense here. That or the guys were punking him, but he thought they were too into the whole ghost-hunting thing to make fun of it like that.

"That doesn't happen." Blaine shook his head. "You guys must have misunderstood me."

"I guess we'll find out when we play the tape back later. Meantime are you picking anything up in here like the other day?" He was of the opinion Blaine was more than just picking up words and feelings, but had been possessed. But he'd wait and see what the cameras had to say before pressing his argument, because God only knew they hadn't picked up much Friday when they'd had the previous great ghost experience.

They all looked at Blaine expectantly.

"There's a definite cold spot in two different areas, and I'm feeling tingling on my right arm over here."

"Have you heard anything from any of them? Is it the nurses? Did she try to help you again?"

"Is it you, Renee? Maryann?" Blaine shivered and rubbed his arms. "Is the meter showing the temperature dropping?"

"Fuck yes." Flynn shivered. "Not to mention my skin is telling the same tale." He grabbed the laptop with the infrared and held it up. "I can see something!" There were definite shapes, three of them.

"Where? Where? What is it?" Blaine turned around, searching the room.

"Right here. It's like they're surrounding us. You can't see anything?" Why couldn't Blaine see them?

Today seemed all assbackwards and weird—weirder than usual anyway.

"I... I feel cold. I...." Blaine's hand raised and turned over. And it didn't look like Blaine was doing it himself.

"Blaine? Should we go, or are you okay?"

"I'm.... Are you looking for my pulse?"

"Of course, honey. Don't worry, I'm here to help."

Flynn gasped, the voice as clear as you please. "Oh God. I heard that. Did you get it, Darnell?"

"Mic's on. Don't know what it's picking up."

Blaine wasn't watching him, wasn't paying attention to them at all. Blaine was looking at someone else.

Flynn had to admit this was far creepier than if he'd seen a specter himself—watching Blaine's unfocused eyes, the way he was communicating with someone who wasn't actually there.

"What do we do, Jase?" he whispered. "Do we stop this?"

"Fuck no," Jason said into the earphone. "Let it run."

Flynn didn't like it. What if something bad happened to Blaine? It didn't seem right to stand aside and let it happen, to do nothing more than watch.

He took a deep breath—if Blaine appeared to be fading or being hurt, Flynn would interfere.

Blaine nodded, like he was answering a question, like he was having a conversation.

"Blaine? Blaine, man, what are you seeing?" Jason asked.

Darnell shook his head. "You gotta talk to us, man. Tell us what you're seeing. Tell the audience what you're seeing."

Flynn strained to see anything, to hear anything, but he didn't. He'd only heard that one sentence and felt the cold, whereas Blaine was clearly communing.

Blaine looked over his shoulder, blinked. "David, don't you think we should get out of here and let these folks do their jobs?"

Blaine was looking right at him, like right into his eyes. This was that possession thing again, because his name wasn't David.

"Blaine? Honey, are you in there?" He stepped forward and reached out, returning his hand to Blaine's arm. His fingers were immediately chilled, and he felt like he'd been hit with high voltage, a shock going all through him and leaving him gasping.

Blaine stepped back, and all of a sudden, a door slammed shut behind him. Flynn jumped about a foot off the ground, and Will swore loudly.

Okay, that was probably just the wind, but damn. Creepy as fuck.

"I suppose we should check the door out? See what made it close?" Flynn would be more than happy if the guys shot down his suggestion.

"Yeah. Yeah, that was fu— screwed up."

Well, that sounded like normal Blaine. Flynn met his gaze, and sure enough, Blaine looked back at him. Actual Blaine actually looking at him. Seeing this now, there was definitely a difference from earlier. And that was maybe creepier than anything else.

"Okay. To the self-closing doors we go. Are we taking bets on what we think it was?" Flynn tried to keep it light.

"I'll take the wind for five bucks," muttered Will, coming closer as they moved slowly forward.

In fact they were all staying much closer to each other than they had so far. Flynn was glad he wasn't the only one who was a little freaked out.

"I'm going with sprung door hinge," Blaine said, while Darnell popped up with some bullshit about a rabid weremoose.

"Kids playing a prank," Will said.

Jason snorted. "Are we really none of us going to say ghosts? I mean, that's why we're here, right? Well, I'm going to put my money on that."

Despite his brave words, Jason was sticking as close to the group as the rest of them. Flynn had the incredibly strong urge to grab Blaine's hand and hold on. In fact he even reached out to do it before he yanked his hand back to his side and told himself not to be a giant pussy.

It was Blaine who grabbed the door handle and turned it, then pulled it with a steady, long tug. It creaked, the sound almost shuddering, almost breaking the air.

Dust poured off the top, showering down around Blaine, and Flynn was fascinated for a second by the sparkle as the sun hit it.

So fascinated that he almost missed it when the door began to fall off the hinges, heading right for Blaine.

Almost.

"Blaine!" He leaped forward and pushed Blaine out of the way, his arm going up to protect his head as the door continued its downward trajectory.

The door was heavy, but not enough to bring him down. Blaine grabbed the edge, and so did Darnell, heaving the door up and out.

"I'd say that makes you the winner, Blaine." Flynn rubbed his arm, glad it hadn't hit his head. Even more glad it hadn't been any heavier than it was.

"Jesus. Are you okay? That was fucked up. God, it could have killed us."

"Yeah." He rolled his neck and his shoulder. He was going to be sore later, but he was okay. "I'm good. So. Broken hinge, not a ghost. We gonna stay here in the emergency room or go upstairs?"

"I think we should review what we got on film."

"You want to leave while we're having a hot streak?" Jason asked, sounding confused.

Flynn backed Blaine up, though. It had been damn weird earlier, and if Blaine needed a break, he was all for it. "We could go refill on water and grab a snack and everything too."

"Whatever. I mean, Flynn almost got hurt, man." Will sounded worried, and they all looked over at him. "I'm freaked the fuck out."

Flynn took a deep breath, feeling suddenly way better hearing someone else say out loud how super creepy this whole thing was. "I'm fine, but I wouldn't be upset if we called it a day either." He could totally hang out with Blaine some more in a non-ghosty situation.

"You guys…," Jason started, but this time it was Blaine who shook his head.

"Seriously, Jase. I'm done. I mean it. I need a break. I have a shit headache coming on."

"That's a majority of three," Will noted. "Let's go."

Flynn chuckled, but he was more than ready to jump on that. He put his arm around Blaine, hoping it wasn't too forward in front of the guys. "Man, you are like an icicle."

"I don't feel so good, man. Seriously. I might hurl."

"Okay, I've got you. See if you can hold it till we're outside." Because barf sitting forever inside the hospital was just going to make everything super gross.

He hurried Blaine ahead of the guys, not running, but definitely moving Blaine along, because just thinking about it made him feel a little like barfing himself.

He got them outside, where the sun was just beginning to set, and guided Blaine to a section of broken pavement off the main sidewalk up to the building. "Just bend over a bit and take deep breaths."

"Right. Right." Blaine sucked in air once, then again.

Flynn rubbed Blaine's back, trying to comfort and help warm him up at the same time. "You are seriously icy."

"Yeah. I feel jittery as hell."

"Guys? Somebody got some water and a cookie or something?" Flynn asked.

"Heads up!" Will tossed him a water bottle, which he managed to catch before it beaned Blaine in the head.

The energy bar Darnell tossed landed on Blaine, and Flynn rolled his eyes as he bent to pick it up.

"Buttheads."

"We're just being helpful."

Flynn guided Blaine over to the van and helped him sit. He gave him the water bottle first, then opened the power bar and offered it to him. "Eat too. You look like a ghost yourself, you've gone so pale."

"I don't know if I can. I'm queasy."

"How about just a tiny bite?" Flynn pulled the bar apart, offering Blaine a little piece of it.

"Thanks. I'll just take a wee bit, right?"

"Just a nibble and see if it helps. If it doesn't, you don't have to eat any more." Hell, Blaine didn't have to eat any of it. He was a grown-up. But Flynn was worried about him and would feel better if Blaine was eating and drinking.

The other guys loaded the van, Jason and Darnell going back for the two cameras left on the second floor as Will played Tetris with the equipment.

Blaine took a few bites, then leaned against Flynn, eyes closed.

"I need to get you home, baby." The words came to him as easy as breathing. "Need to get you away from this place."

He put his arm around Blaine's shoulders and held on tight.

"Baby? You two are in baby mode now? Seriously?" Jason looked a little peeved.

Flynn's cheeks heated, and it annoyed the fuck out of him. What did Jason care where they were? Besides, he was feeling rather protective of Blaine right now.

"Leave him be. We're all wigged," Blaine muttered.

"Yeah, yeah, we are." Darnell nodded and tossed his handful of equipment into the back of the van before coming around and sitting on the other side of Flynn, leaving the front passenger seat for Jason.

"That's what we get for running three times in a row, huh?" Will asked.

"A bigger hit than ever? Maybe we should always do that," Flynn suggested. His heart wasn't in it, though.

Something had felt so off, so wrong. Dangerous, even? That couldn't be what the guys usually experienced when they went out hunting. He'd have to ask Blaine. Once they were far away from here and Blaine was feeling 100 percent himself again, that was.

He breathed a sigh of relief when Will started the engine and they drove away from the hospital.

He swore the shadows followed them all the way down the driveway, and he didn't let go of Blaine. He thought it said a lot that Blaine made no move to pull away from him either.

He didn't really start to relax until they were back on the highway and almost home.

Chapter Seven

THE guys left while Blaine was inside tossing his cookies, and by the time he'd taken a shower and brushed his teeth, Flynn was standing in his room with two steaming cups of fragrant tea.

"Thought this might go down nicely."

"Yeah. Yeah, thank you."

Flynn sat on his bed. "It's peppermint. Should be easy on your stomach." Flynn looked at home in his room.

"You rock." Blaine sat next to Flynn, took the cup, and sipped. "I'm sorry about that."

Flynn shook his head. "It's okay. That was some freaky shit going on back there, and you were right in the middle of it."

"Yeah. Truly. I mean, that was intense." Way more intense than he'd experienced before.

"Have you ever felt anything like it?" Flynn asked, hand on Blaine's thigh.

"No. I don't remember much. Just nausea and being cold."

"You were saying stuff. And talking to someone. And it was like the ghosts were in you. It sounds silly now, but it felt like you were possessed or something." Flynn shrugged. "I told you it was silly. I don't know. Can we talk about something else?"

"Sure, why not? We can talk about all the things, right?" Blaine needed some downtime, something chill.

"Yeah. Yeah, so what do you do in your spare time?" *Tell me about yourself.*

"Bad movies. I mean *bad* movies. The worse they are, the happier I am."

"Yeah?" Blaine drank more tea and let himself lean against Flynn. "I have a TV in here."

"Oh yeah? Netflix has a lot of bad movies on it, and I have an account." Flynn grinned. "We could lie in bed and watch… if it's okay that I'm kind of co-opting your bed."

"It's more than okay. We can be lazy and spend the evening in bed like schlubs." That sounded like more fun than he'd had in months.

"I like it." Flynn smiled at him. "I like you."

"Thank you." Thank God tomorrow was a day off.

Flynn got up and grabbed all the pillows, then set them up at the head of the bed in a pile for them to lie against. "Ta-da!"

"Let me grab the remotes." Blaine dug through the nightstand, then tossed them over.

"So there's one for the TV and one for the cable box, and this last one is for the Blu-Ray, and that's where you get your Netflix?" Flynn perused the buttons as he asked.

"Yep. One day I'll get one of those master mega things, but for now, this works." Hell, he was grateful for satellite in the barn. Dad had laughed his ass off when they'd installed it.

He needed the Wi-Fi, though, for the ghost hunting. The internet was their friend. And it wasn't like he was out at clubs and parties every night. He didn't really consider it a luxury.

"Okay, let's see what bad movies we can find." Flynn already had the remotes figured out and was busy running them.

"I love a man who knows his way around technology."

Flynn grinned. "Then I'm your man." There was something a little extra in Flynn's eyes that said he wasn't really joking.

Blaine let it drop, because it was time to be logical, time to ride the fact that they enjoyed each other's company.

Flynn found them something called *Babylon A.D.* "This has the added bonus of being a Vin Diesel film. He could read me the phone book and I'd be drooling."

"Oh yeah. He's got the voice, huh?"

"Uh-huh. There's something sexy about a man who can rock the bald too. It's not for everyone, but he wears it well." Flynn shifted, leaned against him.

"I don't think I could do it. I like my hair."

"God no. It would totally change your whole vibe. The long hair suits you."

It felt good knowing that Flynn had looked, that he had an opinion on the matter.

"Thanks." Blaine inhaled, filling his lungs, then exhaled, letting the breath relax him.

The movie was entertaining, and Vin Diesel was easy on the eyes. Better than that was the heavy, warm weight of Flynn lying against him.

The tension from earlier today began to ease, began to lift from his shoulders. It helped that Flynn didn't start asking him questions. In fact, they hadn't talked about it at all since they'd gotten home and Flynn had hustled him inside, telling the guys to go get some sleep; they could meet up Monday or Tuesday to look at what they had and discuss the day's work.

He didn't want to talk about it right now, or think about it. He dozed, blinking nice and slow. He wasn't sure what happened during the last half of the movie, but all of a sudden the credits were rolling and Flynn was nuzzling into his neck, breath warm on his skin.

"Mmm." He pulled the blankets up higher, covering them.

"You feeling up to a little fun?" Flynn asked. "Getting reacquainted?"

"Something slow and lazy and fuzzy?"

"Yeah, yeah. Exactly." Flynn smiled and licked at his lower lip, all smiles, a happy sensuality shining in his eyes.

Blaine reached out, wrapped his fingers around Flynn's hip, and petted him in lazy circles. Flynn hummed at his touch and pushed closer.

"Why didn't we strip before lying down?" Flynn asked, fiddling with the bottom of Blaine's T-shirt to get to skin.

"We were being classy?" Blaine tried.

Flynn giggled, the sound light and easy, surprising out of such a strong body. "Classy. I love it."

"Uh-huh. Classy. You and me, classy ghost discoverers."

"I like it. I'm not sure how we make out classily, though. It's inherently messy and unclassy." Flynn had found the skin of Blaine's belly and stroked gently, fingertips dancing on his abs.

"I'm pretty sure that classy making out would be fun, but I think we should just make out like us."

"Do we have a style already?" Flynn asked, eyes twinkling.

Blaine thought maybe they did. Slow and easy, sweet and happy.

"We will after this time, right? Two times is a pattern."

"Works for me. I hope we're good at it."

"At making out?" From what he remembered from their session before, he thought they were pretty damn decent at it.

"Yeah. I want our style to be awesome." Flynn grinned at him. "Like, outstanding."

"Well, if it's not, it means more practice."

"Oh yeah. Yeah. Good point." Flynn laughed and kissed him, the lovely sound filling Blaine's mouth.

He found himself laughing back, pushing right into the kiss and going with it.

Flynn's laughter slowly faded as their kiss deepened, soft little moans sounding in its place. Flynn was warm and sensual, body moving fluidly, and Blaine was so glad to be awake, to be alive and home and not in that hospital.

This was so much better it wasn't even funny.

Flynn got Blaine's shirt pushed up to his underarms, and his fingers wandered across Blaine's chest until they found his right nipple. Then they stayed there, rubbing gently. He loved how Flynn touched him, like the man knew him, understood him.

Flynn shifted to lie next to him, then began opening his jeans, tugging at the button, then pulling down the zipper, fingers protecting his cock, which was filling, demanding attention.

"Oh." Flynn gasped softly as he touched Blaine's cock. "God, I want to suck you."

"I…. Yeah? I'm all over that." As in totally.

"Cool." Flynn wriggled down beneath the covers and tugged Blaine's jeans downward.

They got caught up on his legs, Flynn finally giving up on them.

"Let's… come on. Let's strip down. We have all night."

"Yeah? Okay. Just a second." Flynn's nose slid along his cock, and he could hear him breathing in deeply. Then Flynn took a quick lick before popping up from under the covers. "Okay. Undressing. You're very distracting, and things are, like, stuck. So…."

Flynn climbed out of bed and pulled off his T-shirt, then tugged off his jeans and his underwear, getting naked. Flynn was tall and had great muscles. Nothing gun-showy or anything like that, but enough definition to be pretty damn hot.

"I like that." Blaine could explore for a long few minutes, no question.

"You like what?" Flynn asked, moving closer.

"The way you look. All lean and needy."

"Oh." Flynn's cheeks colored a little, but he smiled and came closer. "Your turn."

"Right." Hell, he'd forgotten he wasn't naked already.

Smiling, Flynn tugged off Blaine's T-shirt, then yanked his jeans the rest of the way down, his underwear going with it. "Oh. Better. God, I like what I see. A whole lot."

Blaine flexed and posed. He looked like a guy who worked a physical job, kept himself clean, and took care of himself. He wasn't anything to sneeze at.

Flynn's eyes lit up, and he climbed onto the bed and began to explore Blaine's body, fingertips sliding down his chest and leaving trails of pure tingles.

Groaning, Flynn leaned in and licked at Blaine's right nipple, then wrapped his lips around it and sucked.

Thank God for oral lovers. Blaine arched under Flynn and pressed up into that hungry mouth. Flynn didn't abandon his touches, but the tingling strokes faded into the background as Flynn's mouth drove him crazy.

He groaned, trying to touch back, but he couldn't figure out how to make his hands work. Flynn seemed happy with soft petting on his head, each moan of approval making Blaine's nipple vibrate between Flynn's lips.

"God, that feels insane. So good."

"I won't stop, then." Smiling, Flynn rubbed his lips back and forth across Blaine's nipple.

"Don't stop. Please." Blaine moaned deep in his chest, the tension beginning to build in his balls.

"I won't stop. You taste too good."

Oh. Tasting. "Want to suck you. We could sixty-nine, get each other off."

He felt Flynn's smile on his skin, then heard it in Flynn's voice. "I love the way you think."

"Come on, then, before I get distracted."

Flynn laughed, but he turned around, lying next to Blaine with his cock right there at Blaine's mouth. Before he could get it between his lips, Flynn's mouth closed over his cock. He twisted his neck, lips parted as he searched for the tip of Flynn's erection. It brushed his lips, and then he caught hold of it, causing Flynn to cry out around Blaine's cock.

Go him for not being a greedy jackass.

Flynn's suction increased, his head bobbing slowly, taking more and more of Blaine in. He flicked Flynn, somehow knowing that he loved pressure around the tip, at the slit. Flynn groaned, hips pushing, sending his hard cock deeper into Blaine's mouth.

Blaine wrapped his fingers around the base, controlling the thrust and giving Flynn everything, sensation all along his prick.

Flynn pulled off Blaine's cock to moan and cry out, "Oh God!" Then Flynn took the head of Blaine's cock back in, sucking hard.

Blaine's toes curled, and he redoubled his efforts, wanting to make Flynn fly. Every sweet cry translated to vibrations around his cock that settled in his balls. Then Flynn took a move right out of Blaine's playbook, tongue-slapping the top of his cock.

Together they were going to drive each other out of their minds. No question. He'd never had a lover he wanted so much.

Flynn kept sucking and slapping, then cupped Blaine's balls and rolled them gently.

Blaine lifted his head, swallowing hard, taking more of Flynn's cock than he had before, throat clenching around the tip. Flynn's suction increased, became stronger but also wilder, telling Blaine he was doing something right.

Flynn grabbed hold of his hip in one hand and played with his balls with the other, both hands clumsy now.

Tentatively, carefully, he tapped Flynn's hole, teasing it, waiting for his response. Flynn pushed his cock deeper again, and his low cry was muffled by Blaine's cock.

Hell yes. He repeated the rhythm—suck, tap, swallow; suck, tap, swallow. Soon the suction on his cock became softer, Flynn's focus clearly shot. The whimpers that vibrated his prick got louder, though, and came more often.

That felt so fucking good. So fucking hot. And he pulled harder, sucked harder.

Flynn pulled off. "Blaine! Blaine! Oh God. Soon."

He nodded and pulled Flynn in deep, swallowing hard as he eased one finger into Flynn's hole. Seed splashed on his tongue and flowed into his mouth. Flynn tasted good—salty and bitter and clean. He approved.

Blaine gentled his suction as soon as Flynn's thrusts slowed, easing his lips back.

"Oh God. That was amazing. Thank you. Oh! Sorry, sorry, I came off. Sorry." Flynn's lips came back onto his cock, sliding along his flesh.

"Uhn…." That was a good enough answer, right?

Flynn didn't seem at all put out by his lack of anything else to say, finding a good rhythm right away, sucking him like a master.

Blaine whimpered and tossed his head. "Don't stop."

Flynn made a noise, and the suction increased; he didn't stop. Thank God.

Blaine's balls ached, his cock throbbing on Flynn's tongue. Flynn rolled his balls again, a little more focused now, really manipulating them. Flynn was more focused with his tongue too, using it to play Blaine's slit.

That was… perfect. Perfect, like they'd been loving each other for years, not minutes.

Flynn kept it up, and Blaine's orgasm drew closer, his ability to think disappearing as the waves of pleasure pushed everything else aside.

"Gonna." That was all the warning he got out before he was shooting, coming hard.

Flynn didn't miss a beat, swallowing again and again. Blaine could feel Flynn's throat closing around the tip of his cockhead.

That was all he could bear, all he could take, and his balls emptied themselves in a rush.

Flynn licked him clean, humming and sucking gently before coming off and slowly kissing his way up Blaine's body. Flynn stopped at his navel, licked around it, then inside it. As he continued, he stopped to kiss each nipple, lips warm, the touches so gentle.

"Hey." Blaine couldn't stop smiling.

"Hey." Flynn rested heavily against him and brought their lips together. The kiss was lazy, sloppy even, but it was easy and sexy, and Blaine could taste himself in Flynn's mouth, knew Flynn could taste himself in Blaine's. And that was pretty damn sexy.

His energy was returning, his balance back. They continued to kiss, touching base with their lips again and again. Then Flynn put his head on Blaine's shoulder and snuggled up close. "I hope we can do that again."

"Maybe after supper, huh? We can throw a couple frozen pizzas in the oven."

"That sounds nice and easy. Which is perfect." Flynn grinned. "Pizza and another bad movie to mock?"

"Hell to the yeah." Oh, he felt hip now.

Flynn laughed, crawled out of bed, and stretched, giving him an amazing view. "I'll go put the pizzas in?"

"Yeah, and I'll pick another movie. There's sausage, pepperoni, meat lovers, and cheese. I'll take whatever."

"Ooh, sausage." Flynn waggled his eyebrows before grabbing his jeans and pulling them on commando.

"Careful with that zipper, now."

Flynn chuckled. "My mini-me thanks you for your concern."

"Your mini-me is on my to-do list." Wait. Was that dorky?

"You should make it a daily to-do." Flynn's cheeks had color, but his eyes were twinkling.

"A repeating task, huh?"

"Yep. That would be a good idea. I think."

"I approve. Seriously." It felt fucking good to have his dorkitude taken as something funny, not stupid.

"Cool. I'll get those pizzas in the oven." Flynn's gaze lingered until he was gone.

Huh. Okay. Okay, this was cool. It was. Unexpected, but cool.

He went through the movies, looking for something that Flynn would consider the right kind of bad.

Oh, *Psycho Beach Party*. Perfect.

By the time he had the movie set up, Flynn was back, cuddling with him. "Twenty minutes to food."

"I picked a super silly one for us."

"Cool. You wanna wait until the pizza is ready before we start it? We could… uh. You know, do stuff."

"You mean neck?"

"That's the one." Flynn grinned.

"Rock on. I'll start." He pounced and nuzzled right into Flynn's neck, blowing a raspberry straight off.

Flynn's laughter echoed around the room; then Flynn pushed him down and tickled his belly, making him cackle.

They rolled together, laughing and rubbing and sharing kisses. It felt natural and right. Like the easiest roommate ever.

"Not just a roommate."

It wasn't an internal thought; the words whispered through his bedroom.

He stilled. "Did you hear that?"

"Hear what?" Flynn asked, head popping up from his neck. Flynn looked around, then back at him. "What?"

"Nothing. I thought I heard a whisper. Must have been the wind."

"Yeah? You sure your barn isn't haunted?" Flynn asked, clearly teasing.

"Pretty damn sure, yeah." Dork.

"Maybe the ghost hitched a ride with us from the hospital." Flynn made a face. "Okay, pretend I didn't say that."

"I've never had that happen, you know."

"What?" Flynn asked, resting his hands on Blaine's chest and his chin on his hands.

"Had a ghost hitch a ride."

"Is that what happened back at the hospital? Someone tried to hitch a ride?"

"I don't think so. I mean, I didn't feel anything in the van." Thank God.

"I mean, while we were in the hospital. It seemed like there was a ghost using you to communicate. Has that happened before?" Flynn asked.

"No, never." And he was pretty sure he didn't want it to happen either. Creepy.

"I didn't like it. It was like you weren't there."

"Hopefully it was just a fluke." Because Blaine didn't remember not being there.

"Is it wrong that we're ghost hunters, but we're hoping not to have an encounter like that again?"

"We're hoping to have some cool things on film more than anything, right?"

"Yeah, the camera better have caught something. Otherwise we're going to look like a whole bunch of scaredy-cats who got spooked at a little bit of darkness."

"Well, part of that is a thing, isn't it? I mean, there's a lot of showmanship, right? In and among the truth?"

"Yeah, I guess. It didn't look like you were putting shit on at the hospital today, though."

"It didn't feel like I was either."

"Cool. Well, if it happens again, I'm going to try and pull you out of it again." Flynn looked deadly serious.

"I think I was just tired. I don't like the idea of...." Of what? Possession? Did he even believe in that?

"You were exhausted." A shiver went through Flynn. "Anyway. We all came home safely."

"Right. That's the important part." Was not coming home safely an option?

"Yeah." Flynn kissed his hand. "I better check on those pizzas. You want a Coke or something to drink?" Flynn was still lying on him, making no attempt to actually get up.

"We still have a few minutes, don't we?" Suddenly he didn't want to be alone.

"Yeah, I'm sure we do." Flynn dropped another kiss on his hand, then leaned up and kissed his lips. "I bet we can take as long as we want. There were more pizzas."

"Or I could wander down with you, rescue them."

"Sure thing. I just thought we were...." Flynn chuckled. "I wanted more sex. Can you blame me? Look at you."

"I want more too. I just... I'm hungry too, and a little wigged."

"Oh man. Call me Mr. Insensitive. I'm sorry. I shouldn't have brought the whole crap at the hospital up. We could have talked about it tomorrow. I wasn't planning to bring it up until we went through the stuff we got on the equipment."

"Hey, it's cool. We're still super new at... everything together."

"Yeah, yeah, we are. But…." Flynn shrugged as they made their way down the stairs. "It's probably silly, but I feel like I've known you forever. I got comfortable with you faster than I ever do with anyone."

"Me too. It's like we're old friends."

"More than friends."

There was that voice again.

"Yeah, exactly. Maybe we knew each other in a former life." Flynn waggled his eyebrows and laughed.

"Maybe. Maybe you were my girlfriend!" Blaine teased.

"Why was I the girl?" Flynn wanted to know.

Blaine noticed that neither of them was pooh-poohing the idea of them having known each other in a former life.

"Maybe we were both girls."

"Oh, I hadn't even thought of that. I like it." Flynn bent over and checked the pizzas through the glass window in the oven. "I think they could use a few more minutes."

"You want water? Milk? Coke?"

"Oh, pizza needs Coke, not milk." Flynn grinned and leaned against the counter, hair mussed around his head, beautiful muscles shining in the kitchen lights.

"Is a can okay?"

"No. I want five-star service, man." Flynn grinned like he was the funniest guy in the world.

"Too fucking bad." Blaine grinned back. He had to.

"Damn. Okay, I'll take a can." Flynn's laughter bounced around the kitchen, making the place feel full of life.

"I'm glad you're here, man." He wouldn't have wanted to spend tonight alone.

"Yeah, me too." Flynn opened his Coke and took a mouthful. "And I'm glad you're not the no-eating-in-bed type."

"I'm easy, for the most part. I've been lonely."

Flynn came over and hugged him tight. "I've got you, babe. Oh God, that's a line from a Sonny and Cher song."

"Dude, it scares me that you know that."

"I shouldn't tell you that I could sing you the entire song, then, should I?"

"No shit?" Well, he knew Flynn was an odd duck.

"I know. Sad, isn't it?" Flynn grinned, shrugged. "I have a knack for remembering all manner of things. Lyrics I'm especially good at. Not a terribly useful skill, except when it comes to tests."

"Hey, that's cool. I wish I tested better. I'm an average student, really. Was."

"Was there something that you didn't get to do because you didn't have better grades?"

"I just didn't have the grades for a full ride, so when the money dried up and Mom and Dad needed me here, here I came."

"At least you're getting to pursue the ghost hunting."

"I am." Right. Quit being all long-in-the-mouth stupid psycho because you don't get every single thing you want.

Flynn gave him a wry smile. "Tell me to shut up if I'm being too Pollyanna for you. I just always try to look for the good in situations, even when they're pretty dire. It's the only way I was able to go forward, you know?"

"Sure. Sure. I'm just a bit of a Debbie Downer sometimes. Stupid, because I'm a lucky bastard."

"Pollyanna and Debbie Downer—doesn't that make us the perfect opposites-attract pair?" Flynn grinned and bumped their hips together just as the timer on the oven went off.

Flynn opened the oven door and bent to check the pizzas. "They're looking just about perfect."

"Good deal. Don't burn yourself." He remembered when David had done that, grabbed a hot pad with a hole and burned his palm bad enough that the blister had been huge.

"Pass me the oven mitts, then." Flynn reached back without looking.

"You got it." He put two in Flynn's hands. "They smell good. There's nothing like a cheap frozen pizza, somehow."

"Does anyone from town deliver out this far?" Flynn pulled the pizzas out and set them on top of the stove.

"God, I wish. No. This is a no-man's land as far as that goes. Hell, my folks are very farm-to-table, you know? Every so often I head to town to Burrito Gringo, just because."

Flynn laughed. "I love Mexican. And they do huge burritos there. Huge everything, really. It's a good deal." Flynn made short work of slicing the pizzas and dishing them onto large plates. "I do love the farm-to-table movement, though."

"Oh, it's the only reason that we're still in business, but sometimes I want to be that guy in a loft downtown near the clubs and drinking coffee in crazy little shops." He grabbed forks and napkins. "Seriously, I'd last about a day and a half and be utterly overwhelmed and wanting to come home."

"I've been to some clubs." Flynn made a face. "Too loud. And some of the gyrations that get called dancing...." Shaking his head, Flynn laughed again. "They always called me old-fashioned at university. Just because I'm not into the club scene!"

"I don't imagine I am either, but I sort of wish I was. I want to be cooler than I am."

Flynn stopped, literally frozen where he was, eyes on Blaine. "I think you're pretty damn cool, Blaine. I know I'm only one guy, but... no fooling, you're the coolest guy I know."

Oh. Oh okay. That felt like.... It felt like the best thing he'd ever heard. "Thanks. Seriously. That rocks."

"You're welcome—just telling it like it is." Flynn grabbed his plate and his Coke and they headed back upstairs. "Did I tell you how cool it is that you're not afraid to let us eat on your bed?"

"You might have mentioned it. I take it you had a guy who was?"

Flynn snorted. "That's like saying that the center of the sun is a little bit hot. Hell, some days I was lucky Dirk let me eat at the dining room table. When he was home alone, he'd eat holding his plate over the kitchen sink. He had this real phobia about crumbs leading to bugs. I never did get out of him what bad experience he'd had with bugs as a kid, but I always figured it had to be something really traumatic."

"That sucks—for you and him, huh? I mean, I can't imagine." Bugs were a part of farm life.

"Yeah. I felt sorrier for him than me in the end. I mean, I got to leave and go roll in the mud or something and not worry about it. He was germaphobic, bugaphobic, dirtaphobic. He had to have everything just so, and his entire place was white so he could see if there were crumbs or bugs or any sort of dirt. He tried seeing a therapist for it, but that never took."

"Well, you can sort of tell that's not me...." Sort of. Like a lot.

"No, you have a much cooler vibe. Relaxed. Easy. Not that I'm saying you're easy! Just… you know what I meant, right?"

God, Flynn really was a giant dork. It was kind of hugely adorable.

"I am, though. Easy. And weirdly happy and embarrassed about it."

Flynn laughed and put his food on the bed, then took Blaine's from him and set that down as well. That done, Flynn wrapped him in a hug and kissed him. It was the easiest thing on earth to hold on, to wrap his arms around Flynn and kiss right back.

Their mouths parted, though Flynn didn't back off, and when he spoke, his lips tickled Blaine's. "I like you easy, and you don't have to be embarrassed about it. I've proved to be pretty easy myself, at least when it comes to you."

"I like it. Lots. Let's eat." He was suddenly ravenous.

"Yeah, 'cause God knows I can't jump your bones while there's pizza on the bed. I mean, eating in bed is one thing, rolling all over the food is another."

"Yeah. Hot cheese burns delicate bits." He spoke from experience.

Flynn laughed again as he threw himself down on the bed, making their plates bounce. It was a damn good thing he'd put the Cokes on the side table and not the mattress.

Settled against the pillows, Flynn looked totally at home in Blaine's bed.

Blaine moved more carefully, settling down and starting the movie before grabbing his pizza. Flynn shifted once he'd settled, moving so they were touching from shoulders to hips and from hips to ankles.

"I like this," he whispered. He liked it a lot.

"Me too. It's…." Flynn shrugged. "I don't know. I'm not the word guy; I'm the science guy. I was lonely too. And that makes it sound like I'm here just because I was lonely, and that's not it at all. Maybe that's why I thought renting a room from you was such a great idea, but it's not why I'm here"—Flynn pointed at the bed—"with you."

"We'll figure out the why part, right?"

"Yeah, we will. I just don't want you thinking any port in a storm is why I'm here."

"I don't know. That's sort of heroic on my end. Being Mister Porty McStorm?"

Flynn giggled, nearly choking on his bite of pizza.

Blaine winked, feeling clever as hell. Flynn was definitely good for his ego.

After Flynn swallowed, he leaned up and kissed the corner of Blaine's mouth.

It was sweet and gentle, just about perfect, and he thought he could get used to it. Flynn smiled at him, then turned his attention back to his pizza and took another bite. He kept shooting little smiles at Blaine, happy little glances.

It felt good, and more than that, it felt safe somehow.

When they'd finished their pizzas, Flynn wiped the grease from his mouth and leaned his head against Blaine's shoulder.

Yeah, this had possibilities. This worked.

Chapter Eight

THE guys were all otherwise busy on Monday, so Flynn and Blaine checked the footage together. Flynn could barely keep from bouncing as they waited for it to load. He'd heard things. He'd seen things. And Blaine had been freaking possessed. Surely they had something on film to show for their weird visit to the hospital on Sunday.

Still, other than a couple of strange lights that seemed to be on Blaine's shoulders, there was nothing.

Nothing.

How could that be?

He looked at the tape, rewound it, watched it again. Then he gaped at Blaine. "What the fuck?"

"Is there… are they working right? Is there more footage?"

Flynn shook his head, feeling confused and kind of angry. "That's all of it, and there's something wrong with the sound, because it didn't come through on any of them. I don't know if the mike wasn't plugged in properly, if it's broken, or what, but there's no sound, there's barely any footage that isn't all washed-out. It's like someone sabotaged our equipment."

"Huh. Should we call Jason to test the cameras?"

"That's probably a good idea. I mean, this doesn't even have your narration in it, let alone anything we saw. Get him to check everything, but we were getting temperature changes and EMF readings, so it just seems like the cameras and the mike were messed up. I mean, it could just be a coincidence, but they worked great Saturday when we didn't see or hear shit, so that's a hell of a coincidence." Honestly, Flynn didn't know what to think.

There were a few possibilities. It could have been a fluke, some random equipment failure. It could have been sabotage, either by one of the team or someone who wanted to discredit them. Or it could have been that all the activity they'd had going on had messed with the equipment. What did it say about Flynn that he was hoping it was the last option?

"Maybe the spirits affected them, you know?" suggested Blaine. "They can suck batteries...."

Flynn nodded, pleased that he hadn't been the only one thinking this could have been due to ghostly interference. "Yeah? I was thinking that was a possibility. Of course does that mean anytime we actually make contact our equipment is going to go tits-up? That's not exactly going to help us prove anything, is it?"

"I don't know. That's your job, isn't it? To invent things to fix that issue?"

Flynn laughed and bumped shoulders with Blaine. "It totally is. I guess I'll get Jase to test the equipment, and then we'll have to do tests at the site—different machines, different settings, backups, etc."

"I guess I need to start researching other places to go too, and update the blog with pictures and some video."

"Having a new destination will be great, but I think we're not nearly done with the hospital yet. I mean there's definitely something there, and we haven't even hit the second floor."

Blaine shivered, and Flynn swore that a shadow crossed his face.

"Blaine? You okay, man?" It was almost like when Blaine had been possessed back at the hospital.

"Hmm? Yeah. Yeah, totally. I'm fine."

That didn't sound like the truth.

Flynn bumped their shoulders again. "Come on, man. You can tell me anything. I think I've proved that I'm on your side."

"I… I just don't think we should worry about the second floor. It's dead."

"Yeah? I thought you said there was stuff going on up there. I mean, we went up on that first quick run-through, and then you had the guys put a couple of motion-activated cameras there." Flynn was confused because he was sure it had been on the agenda early Friday.

"I just… it's a bad idea."

He didn't get it. It was almost like Blaine was afraid of going up to the second floor. Which didn't make a whole lot of sense—he was looking for ghosts after all, not trying to avoid them. "Why?"

"Why does there have to be a why? It's a dangerous old hospital, that's all."

"I know, but… I just don't get why we can't give the second floor a try. If we're getting this much activity on the main level, why not look for more upstairs? We can take extra care."

"I'll see. I have to talk to the owners and see if we can go back."

"Somebody owns that place?" Flynn had assumed it was just a condemned building. Maybe owned by the state or something.

"Yeah, a bunch of investors. You know, it's a tax write-off."

"Well, I imagine as long as we've signed a waiver saying if anything happens to us it's on us and not them, they won't care what we do." He was eager to explore more. Now that he'd done it in person, he thought he might be hooked on ghost hunting.

"Maybe. Maybe. There's a couple of places—a hotel that's rumored to be haunted and an abandoned cottage."

"They sound great. We really should do a bunch of tests with the equipment at the hospital, though. I can't really compare filming in one place with filming in another, you know? That would change too many of the variables." It was true, but he was also being stubborn about going back to the hospital because Blaine seemed so determined not to go back, which honestly seemed like a one-eighty. And there was plenty left there for them to explore. Flynn had a strong hunch that they'd only just scratched the surface.

Not only that, but something was wrong. Not with him—with Blaine. Was he overreacting? He didn't know Blaine that well, but…. No, something was wrong. And it had all started on their last visit to the hospital, and they had to go back there to fix it. That much he was sure of.

Flynn stared Blaine down, waiting for him to come up with another explanation for why they shouldn't, or couldn't, go back to the hospital.

Blaine shrugged. "I'll see what I can arrange, okay? I'll talk to Jase."

Flynn shook his head, but he imagined that Jase and the others wouldn't want to give up on what had been a fairly active scene two times out of three. Almost scarily active in fact. So he capitulated. "Yeah, that's fine, man. I'll get this video transferred to the new storage hard drive and get it backed up."

"That sounds great." Blaine rubbed the back of his neck, wincing a little.

"You got a crick?" Flynn laid his hand on Blaine's neck and dug his fingers in, the motion slightly awkward, sitting next to the man as he was. "I could sit behind you and give you a proper massage."

"Just a headache."

Yeah, except there was a hot spot on Blaine's neck, a little swelling.

"Indulge me—I took a massage course at university." Flynn grinned as he shifted behind Blaine. The couch was nice and wide, so there was plenty of room for him to fit between the back of the thing and Blaine without knocking him onto the floor.

Flynn tugged Blaine's shirt back a little so he could get a better look at Blaine's skin.

There was what looked like a bite—not a spider bite, but a human bite—right there where the base of Blaine's neck met his shoulder. And it was definitely warm, inflamed. He didn't like the looks of it.

"Did someone bite you, babe?"

"Did you leave a hickey?"

No. No, this wasn't a hickey. This was a bite.

"Not a hickey. Not me." Flynn ran his fingers gently across it.

"I'm not letting—" Blaine jerked and pulled away. "Ow!"

"Something bit you, Blaine, and it looks like human teeth marks." He wasn't accusing Blaine of anything—hell he'd been with the guy for the last few days, and this bite was brand-new. "It looks infected."

"Weird. Maybe it's a spider. You think I should put some peroxide on it?"

"I think we should do something about it, yeah. But it doesn't look like a spider bite. You got peroxide? I can go get it."

"In the bathroom. Thanks."

He found antibiotic cream, peroxide, a few Tylenol, and a cloth, along with some muscle cream.

Coming back, he again set up behind Blaine, who blinked at all the stuff he'd brought.

"You don't think this is overkill?"

"No, I don't at all." Flynn handed over the Tylenol. "Take two of these."

"Yes, boss." Blaine swallowed them dry.

Flynn shook his head but turned his attention back to the bite. He used the peroxide first. While he held the cloth against Blaine's back beneath the bite, he poured peroxide on the affected area.

Jesus. The liquid bubbled up, white foam developing immediately. He poured more on the bite, wincing. "Does it hurt?"

"It stings."

"It's pretty infected. We're going to need to keep an eye on it. It wasn't there yesterday, I'm sure."

"Weird. I don't remember us getting that wild in the bedroom."

"We didn't. I didn't do this." Frowning, Flynn wiped away the excess liquid and foam. He drizzled on more peroxide, astonished that it was still bubbling up. "We might need to go to the clinic or something."

"I'll see if Mom doesn't have some sort of salve when I see her."

"Well, you had some antibiotic cream. I can put that on it. But it looks pretty nasty, and ten minutes ago it was just a little red and hot." It hadn't seemed so *off* only moments ago, had it? Crazy.

Flynn didn't know what to make of it. He touched it gently, pushing a bit.

Blaine groaned, the sound deep, pained. "Damn, that's sore."

"I'm going to keep a very close eye on it." Flynn poured some more hydrogen peroxide on it. "If it gets any worse, I'm taking you to the doctor."

"Yeah. First, I'll see if Mom has anything to put on it. Later. You want to keep working, or you want to go see what's on TV?"

"If that's a euphemism, I definitely want to go see what's on TV."

"Listen to you!" Blaine chuckled softly but nodded.

"Hey, I can go through film or actually watch TV anytime. Euphemising with you is special." Blaine made him feel warm—not just in his balls, either.

He took one last look at Blaine's neck, then stood and held out his hand. "Come on. Your, uh, TV is waiting."

"Yeah, yeah, yeah." Blaine rolled his neck a little, then took Flynn's hand.

"If you're not feeling up to it...." Flynn didn't want to push Blaine if the guy was hurting.

"Up to TV?" Blaine rolled his eyes, winked.

Laughing, Flynn tugged Blaine up the stairs with him. Okay, it had been a silly question. He was pretty sure Blaine would say yes to a blow job even if he was on his deathbed.

Maybe he'd be able to convince Blaine to go back to the hospital after an orgasm… or two. Flynn had a hunch that they'd have to in order to figure out what the heck was going on.

Chapter Nine

BLAINE'S neck burned like fire.

Mom had smeared it with some stuff she'd made up, but it hadn't helped a bit. It just made the burn deeper, now running all the way to his elbow.

Christ.

He stood in front of the mirror over the dresser, poking at the swollen skin, pushing on it.

There was something there—a hard mass right under the skin.

Flynn came in from the bathroom and stopped short. "Jesus, Blaine. That thing's grown, like, three times its size." Flynn started putting on clothes. "In, like, a day. Get dressed—I'm going to take you to the hospital." Flynn sounded worried, honestly worried.

"I'm fine, seriously. I just…." He pressed again, frowning. "Is there something in there?"

Flynn stood behind him and studied the wound. Then he touched it, pressed against the hard spot. "Jesus. I think it's loaded with pus. I'm serious; we need to get to the hospital and get this dealt with."

He grabbed Blaine's clothes and began handing them over.

Blaine pulled his pants on and then froze as something moved, pulled inside him, inside the bump. "Wait."

"What?" Flynn stared at him, wide-eyed.

"I just…." Blaine pressed again, and his swollen skin split, a foul-smelling goo pouring down his arm. There was something in there. Something… moving. "Flynn! Get it out!"

"Oh fuck." Flynn grabbed his good arm and dragged him into the bathroom. Flynn turned on the hot water in the sink, soaked a washcloth, and dragged it over Blaine's arm, cleaning away the gunk before rinsing it and then pressing it against the split in Blaine's skin to draw out more pus. "Grab me the tweezers, man. Fuck."

"Get it out!" Blaine could feel it. In him.

In me. Oh God. Please.

Flynn reached past him and grabbed the tweezers out of the medicine cabinet. "Fuck. Gross. Shit. Just stay still." He snagged a clean washcloth and ran it under the hot water, then did the same with the tweezers.

When Flynn pressed the cloth against his shoulder, the ache made Blaine cry out. Then Flynn gave a cry of triumph, and Blaine swore he could feel whatever it was being pulled out, slithering and twitching inside him until it was gone.

Flynn threw the thing on the counter, grabbed a water glass, and slammed it onto the—oh my God, it was a *worm*. Jesus Christ, Blaine was going to throw up.

"Oh my God. Oh my God. Please. Please, is that it?" Blaine tore at his shoulder, the pus turning bloody.

"Stop. Just stop." Flynn pushed his hands away. "Wash them. And I mean a lot."

Flynn soaked the cloth again and wiped away the blood and more pus. Then he grabbed the peroxide and poured it over the area once more and blotted the excess liquid with a towel.

"You have to make sure they're all out!" What if there were more? Dozens? Eggs? What if they were squirming inside him and then trying to eat their way out?

Flynn took him by both arms and shook him until his hair flew. "Stop it!" He went silent until Blaine met his eyes in the medicine-cabinet mirror. "It's going to be okay. You are going to put a clean T-shirt on, and I'm going to grab that thing, and then we're going to the hospital. They'll be able to make sure it's cleaned out properly, okay?"

"I-I—it was in me. Fuck." Blaine was going to lose it. He caught sight of the worm, smashed and bloody under his glass. His bathroom glass. "Hurry."

Numb, Blaine obeyed Flynn's instructions, grateful to have someone else taking charge. Flynn seized another cloth and wrapped the bug in it, a visible shudder moving through him. Then he hurried Blaine out to Flynn's car and parked him in the passenger seat.

In seconds they were on the road, Flynn driving way too fast. "You're going to have to tell me how to get to the hospital."

"I…. David. I'm going to be sick." He didn't want to go back. He'd been to the hospital so much, so many times.

Too many times.

"Not in the car, man." Flynn reached in the back and came up with a bag. He dumped out the contents and passed it over. "Here. Here. And who the heck is David?"

"David who? I don't know any Davids."

"You called me David." Flynn shook his head. "Never mind. It doesn't matter. Left or right up here? Left or right?"

"Left. Left." Right? He felt so wigged, like he had a brain fog. Like he was lost.

"Okay. Oh, there's signs now. We've got to be almost there." Flynn's hand landed on his leg and squeezed. "We're almost there, and you're going to be fine. I swear, okay?"

"Room 204."

He looked at Flynn. "What?"

"I said we're almost there, and you're going to be fine. Say something, though, eh? Talk to me? Tell me how it's feeling."

"Better." No. No, Flynn *had* said 204. Hadn't he? "A little numb."

"They'll clean it out and shoot you full of antibiotics, and you'll be right as rain in no time. It'll be fine." Flynn kept saying that like if he repeated it enough times, it would be true.

"Yeah. Except for the whole worm thing, huh? It was alive. What if…?"

"Shh. They'll clean it."

"But—"

"No. Just don't. You'll drive yourself crazy with 'what-ifs.' We don't speculate. Penicillin kills shit like this. We can talk about what the fuck that was after everything's smelling like roses again."

"I swear I can feel them, moving inside me." He swatted at his shoulder, tugging at his shirt.

"Blaine. Lover. You have to stop. Hold on to your hands or something. Just no touching." They turned into the hospital, and Flynn parked as close to the emergency entrance as he could. Then he almost ran Blaine into the ER and over to the nurse at reception.

The fact that they were in the ER of a hospital, albeit a different hospital, and that was where this had all started, did not escape Blaine.

"My friend had this in him." Flynn thrust out the cloth with the squished bug. "And it's all infected, and we're worried there are eggs in there or even other bugs."

"In him?"

"Yes. Here!" Blaine snapped to get the nurse's attention. "Listen to me!" What if they were already in his brain? Floating in his eyeballs?

"Please. You have to look at him right away, make sure they aren't, uh, multiplying in there." Flynn grabbed Blaine, turned him around, and raised his T-shirt. "Look. It's awfully infected."

The nurse's nose wrinkled, and she took a half step back. "Okay. Follow the green line on the floor, and when you get to the nurse there, tell her you're to go into isolation three."

"Yes, ma'am. Thank you. Come on. Come on, Blaine. I'll get hold of your folks. Come on."

Blaine held on to his head, the pounding suddenly huge, damn near unbearable. He let Flynn walk them through the red tape and sank down with a sigh of relief when he was finally able to sit on a bed. Flynn grabbed his phone and made that call to Blaine's folks.

"Someone will be in to clean the infection and start an IV for antibiotics and something for pain," the nurse who'd met them said. "Just sit tight."

Flynn hung up, then came and sat next to him as soon as she left. "Are you feeling worse?"

"My head hurts. I swear, this was…. It was in me."

"I know. It was pretty gross. I didn't think we had bugs like that here."

"I've worked on the farm my whole life. My whole life, man!" He'd never even heard of this shit.

"I think it was the hospital." Flynn peeked at his back and winced.

Before either of them could add anything, another nurse came in and introduced herself as Rose. She put an IV in Blaine's arm, and about two minutes after that, the analgesics kicked in and the pain eased.

Then she began to clean the wound, and Flynn looked away. Blaine didn't blame him. He wouldn't have wanted to watch it either. Especially as she put on gloves and a facemask to do it.

Another nurse popped her head in. "Your parents are here."

"I'll switch with them," Flynn offered. "No problem."

"Don't leave, though. Don't just leave."

"Why would I do that?"

That was a great question. Why would Flynn do that? Why would Blaine worry about it? Why would he even say it?

"I'll be in the waiting room. Is that okay? I mean… I don't have to go, but I don't think they're going to let us all be in here."

Rose nodded. "He's right. One at a time, though we'll make an exception for your parents. For a short time."

"Okay. Okay, thanks. God." He leaned forward, the scent of blood and antiseptic making him want to die. Or barf.

"I'll be in the waiting room if you need me," Flynn said. He glanced at Blaine's back where the nurse was still working. "It's looking better. You're going to be fine."

God, he hoped so. But he wasn't sure. What if they were still in him? What if the bugs were still inside him?

Flynn disappeared, and Blaine's folks came in moments later, his father appearing concerned, his mother fussing hard.

"What the fuck is it, son? When did you notice it?"

"When did I get you to doctor it, Mom?" he asked, the room spinning around him.

"Day before yesterday."

"That morning, Pop. Flynn saw it."

"It wasn't nearly this bad then, though. I would have insisted you go to the hospital if it had looked like this." His mother fussed some more, wincing every time she looked at his shoulder.

"We've cleaned it out," the nurse explained, "and the doctor is coming to lavage it again and suggest some meds to make sure everything's cleared out."

"You can't see any more in there, can you?" Blaine needed to know they were gone.

"The doctor will make sure everything is kosher. And the antibiotics are doing their job."

"Please, just make sure."

"I'm going to see if we can't get you something for anxiety. Does he have anxiety issues, normally?"

"Blaine? Our Blaine?" Mom looked panicked. "God no."

"Okay, Anna, just take a few breaths. He doesn't need *you* having an anxiety attack over this."

"My poor baby…. Your poor shoulder…."

"He's going to be just fine, aren't you, son?"

Blaine looked at his pop, nodded. "Yeah. I mean, I'm here now, right? They know about this stuff?"

"Of course they do. You're going to be fine, son. And we'll get the barn fumigated. Make sure this doesn't happen again."

"Yes, sir." What if it was the hospital, though? Not this one, the other.

He didn't want to go back if it was the hospital. Shit, he didn't want to go back anyway. He needed to keep David safe.

"Room 204."

"Where's Flynn? Is he okay? Where is he?"

"He went to the waiting room so your mother and I could be here." His father patted his hand. "I'll go take a turn in the waiting room and send him back, shall I?"

"They'll send me home soon, right?"

"The nurse said the doctor would be in shortly. I'm sure it won't be much longer. I'll go get your friend, son."

"Thanks, Pop. I'm sorry."

His dad shot him a quicksilver grin. "For what? This will buy me a few cups of joe tomorrow morning, huh?"

That startled a laugh out of Blaine, and his father gave him a wink before heading out.

"Does it hurt, sweetie?" his mom asked, looking at his shoulder and *tsk*ing. "It wasn't nearly this bad yesterday."

"Not now. It's so creepy. What if it's inside me? More of them, I mean?"

"Then the doctor worms you and gets rid of them."

"Mom!"

"What? It works for the dogs...." She gave him a sweet laugh, and he shook his head. She'd always been a proponent of laughter being the best medicine, and it seemed to have worked for her with the cancer, so he couldn't knock it.

"Laughter—that's a good sign," Flynn noted as he walked in. He smiled at Blaine. "You're looking less green around the gills."

"They gave me some stuff." He had the feeling more was coming too. "I was freaked out. That was...."

Just thinking about it made his balls crawl up into his body.

Flynn made a face. "It was the grossest thing I've ever seen. If I never have to pull a worm—uh, do that again, it'll be too soon."

"Yeah." Blaine shivered and rolled his eyes, worried again that it was all going to repeat. That itch and then the bug.... God.

"Hey. Hey, guys!" Mom patted his foot, shook it a little. "Let's not relive it, shall we?"

"I just wish we knew how it happened." Flynn leaned over to look at it. "It looks clean, Blaine. It totally does."

"Uh-huh. Gross. I want the doctor to guarantee me it's over."

"Room 204."

He shook his head. What the fuck?

"Blaine?" Flynn was watching him closely. "Feeling okay?"

"My head is just...."

"They gave him pain meds, huh?" Mom asked. "They always make him a little crazy."

"Ah. It's a good thing I'm rooming at the barn, eh?" Flynn grinned, but Blaine could read the concern beneath the smile.

"Yes. Otherwise he'd be sleeping in his old room."

"Don't worry, Mrs. King. I'll make sure this doesn't happen again. Or if it does, I'll make sure we get back here right away."

"We're going to get the barn fumigated," Mom insisted.

"If that's where it happened." Flynn met Blaine's eyes, and Blaine could see his own doubts in Flynn's.

"Well, where else? You two haven't been exploring anywhere freaky, have you?"

Blaine immediately shook his head. "Nope. Nowhere we haven't been a hundred times."

"That's what I figured. I'm having your father call the exterminator today."

"Are we going to have to go to a hotel for a few days?" Flynn asked.

"Of course not. You boys can both stay at the house with us as long as you need to."

"Thanks, ma'am."

"Oh please, call me Anna." She patted Flynn's arm. "I'm going to go make sure your father is okay. Maybe get some coffee. You boys okay here?"

"We're fine. I've got him. I promise."

Mom looked at Blaine, then at Flynn, and her eyes got wide for a second. She smiled. "Well, good deal. I'm glad of that."

Flynn's cheeks reddened, and he ducked his head. Once Mom was gone, Flynn met Blaine's gaze. "Oh man. She knows."

"She does." She was cool with Blaine being gay. So was Pop. He knew how lucky he was, and he never let himself forget it.

Flynn grinned. "I guess it's real, then, huh? No going back now that the folks know." Flynn moved closer, and the heat from his body seeped into Blaine.

"I'm a little wigged. Promise you'll stay here."

God, he was a needy bastard.

"I'm not going anywhere," Flynn said. "I promise. Especially now that your folks know. I won't feel like they think I'm being a jerk for sticking close and keeping them from being in here with you."

"Room 204."

Seriously, what the fuck?

"Room 204."

"Did you hear that?"

"Hear what, babe?"

"What if there's bugs in my brain? Making me hear things?" What if the hospital was inside him now? What if they were in him? His heart rate began to speed up, the beeping of the monitors getting louder.

"Hey, hey, you're fine. You need to breathe, okay? Take some deep, even breaths. Come on. You gotta relax or you're going to get the staff here all upset."

Sure enough, the nurse came back, frowning at the monitors, then at him.

"I have orders to give him an antianxiety med, and we're going to administer a vermifacient as well."

"A what?" What the hell?

"It's just a precaution."

Flynn had his phone out, but he shrugged. "I'm just seeing mentions of it in medical journal articles." He turned to the nurse. "Is the vermifacient because of the bug? Because if you've got something for that, it would really help set him at ease."

The nurse had pushed the meds into his IV already, and he could feel quiet fall over him like a blanket.

"Yes, exactly. Just in case, we're making sure nothing else is in there."

"There you go. They're on it." Flynn had his hand now, holding on tight and stroking Blaine's knuckles with his free hand.

He found that he didn't really care. He was floating, wrapped in cotton wool.

"That's calmed you down nicely." The nurse's voice sounded like it was coming from a long way away. "The doctor will get to you as soon a she can. In the meantime, your shoulder has been covered, so you can lie back against the pillows and relax."

The sensation of moving was huge. Then all he could see was the ceiling tiles. And Flynn's head. Flynn's huge, disembodied head.

"You're okay, Blaine. It's just the meds."

"Room 204," he muttered. "You have to promise me."

Flynn frowned. "You mean at the hospital? Okay. Okay, I promise. We'll check it out, man."

"No. No more. You can't ever." Never.

"What are you talking about, Blaine?" The bed dipped as Flynn sat next to him, close and warm. "What happened in room 204? Has that got something to do with what's going on?"

"Promise me." He grabbed his lover's hand. "Please, David. I can't lose you again."

Chapter Ten

OH man. Blaine was losing it. Calling Flynn David. Telling him to stay out of room 204 like there was something there. If there was, though, why wouldn't Blaine want them all to go check the room out? Come to think of it, Blaine had been really insistent that they stay off the second floor altogether. Which was weird because on their initial walk-through, Blaine had taken him up there—all that funny echoing of his laughter and voice had filled the hallway and the stairwell. Then Blaine had directed the guys to set up the stop-motion cameras on the second floor. Why would he have done that if he didn't want them in that room?

Flynn had done some looking shit up on his phone while he was in the waiting room too. The bug he'd taken out of Blaine—and fuck, that was still the grossest thing ever—looked like a maggot. The thing was, flies didn't lay their eggs in live flesh, and they didn't lay just a single one. Considering the bite mark had looked human, it was almost as if someone dead had bitten Blaine and transferred the single maggot to Blaine's body that way.

Just thinking about it made him want to throw up a little, so Flynn shook the thoughts from his head and gave Blaine a reassuring smile. "David won't go into room 204. I promise." There. He wouldn't be breaking the promise if they went back to the hospital and wound up checking out room 204—which he was kind of thinking they ought to. The thing was, would Blaine ask him who the hell David was?

"Good. Good. There's nothing but death there. Nothing but death for us."

Flynn didn't know if this was something new or how Blaine always was. It almost felt like Blaine was transmitting something from the other side. He was going to have to ask the guys if anything like this had ever happened with Blaine before. Speaking of the guys, Flynn figured he could ask them what was up with room 204. Had they found anything in their research pertaining to it?

He patted Blaine's good shoulder, then texted the guys. *any research on rm 204? need intel*

Will answered first. *u mean hspital? Ask B*

Flynn rolled his eyes. He totally would if he didn't think all he'd get as an answer was more of that blind panic.

cant. documentation? Surely they had files for everything, and that would contain anything they'd found out about the hospital.

Just in case, he turned back to Blaine and asked carefully, "So… room 204. What's the story there?"

"Story?" Blaine blinked at him. "What story?"

"Yeah. You know, the research. What did it tell you about room 204?" Flynn kept his voice even, not wanting to get Blaine all worked up again. Besides, he didn't think he'd get any info if he got Blaine all het up.

"There's something upstairs. Something sad."

"Oh yeah? Somebody died?" That would make sense—it was a hospital after all. People died there all the time.

"I don't know. They don't talk to me. You can't go up there. It's dangerous."

"Who doesn't talk to you, babe?" He stroked Blaine's belly. "You need to talk to me. You need to tell me who doesn't talk to you and why it's dangerous in room 204."

"You can't go up there. Never ever. That's where you die."

Flynn gasped. "Where I die? Are you prescient too?" Nobody had told him Blaine could tell the future.

"You already did, David. You did, and it's all my fault."

Oh man. David again. Who did Blaine think he was? Who did Blaine think _he_ was?

"Hey. Can you tell me your name?" He asked the question suddenly, hoping to shock Blaine a little.

"Christian." The name fell from Blaine's lips as he dozed off.

Jesus Christ.

Fuckadoodle doo.

And holy shit.

Blaine thought he was someone called Christian and that Flynn was David. What the hell? Was it because of the bug? _Had_ it done something to Blaine's brain? Or was this possession? There had been something odd with Blaine back at the ER in the hospital the other day, like someone else was talking through him.

Flynn's fingers were trembling as he sent another text out. *really need 2 know re rm204 & anyone called Christian or David*

This time Jason answered. *utalkingbout the suicide gay guys?*

Whoa. What? *suicide gay guys????????*

yeah. Long story. Tell you l8r

He hit Contacts on his phone and called Jason.

"I need to know now," he told Jason. "I need the whole story."

"Why? It's ancient. It's like from the eighties, man."

"Because something weird is happening with Blaine, and I need to know the whole story right now. Just tell me, okay?" Flynn touched Blaine's arm, needing the connection.

"Blaine? What's wrong with him? Do you guys need help?"

"We're at the hospital. He's fine. Sedated. Bite gone wrong. I need to know about the suicide gay guys. Were they Christian and David?"

"Bite? You bit him?"

He slapped his forehead.

"Bug bite! Jesus, Jason. Just tell me already."

"Jeez. Okay! There was a dude with brain cancer, and his lover, David, wanted to stay with him, but the family sucked rocks and wouldn't let him. The Christian guy begged and begged, and finally a sister or an aunt or someone smuggled him in, but it was too late. The guy died like minutes before, and the David dude shot himself right there in the room or something. Creepy shit. Romeo and Juliet-y, but not."

"Shit, that's awful. It was room 204 that it happened in, wasn't it? You guys ever get any hits off the room

before?" Was Blaine possessed by Christian's ghost?
Was that what was going on here?

"Uh. Maybe? I mean, I don't really know. We tend
to film downstairs 'cause it's safer."

"Okay. Cool. Cool. Hey, did you see anything bite
Blaine while we were out at the hospital?"

"Like what? Is that why he freaked so bad?"

"I guess. I don't know. But something laid an egg
in there, and it hatched into this ugly... well, it was
gross, and now he's being pumped full of antibiotics
and shit." He didn't want to make more of the whole
thing than it was, but frankly between the bug and
Blaine calling him David and saying his own name was
Christian and there being a suicide gay couple... well,
he was more than a little freaked.

"Ew. Do you need me to come up? I'm at work, but
I'll take off. Darnell's off today, I think."

The offer made him smile. They were a solid
group, good guys. Great friends.

"Nah, his folks are here, and they just gave him
the really good drugs, and he's sleeping. The doc is
supposed to send him home after taking a look at it. I'll
send you a text when they spring him and you could
come over and have some beers."

"Sure. I'll let all the guys know. We'll bring pizza."

"Sounds great. Thanks, man. I'll let Blaine know
when he wakes up. He'll be pleased."

"Sure. Keep me posted." The line went dead, and
Flynn sat there, mind spinning.

What the hell was going on? What the everloving
fuck? Seriously.

Flynn was worried. Big-time. He just hoped that
when Blaine woke up, he knew he was Blaine.

Chapter Eleven

BLAINE felt like cotton-wrapped, hammered shit, but at least he felt like cotton-wrapped, hammered shit at home.

The exterminator had come, pronounced the barn clean, and gone, and he was on his couch, three butterfly bandages on his shoulder and Flynn staring at him like he was going to explode in a ball of pus any moment.

"How are you feeling?" Flynn asked, coming closer.

"Glad to be home. Sorry for all the drama." They'd been at the ER for damn near twenty-four hours.

"That's okay. Hey, how do you spell your name? They were asking at the hospital and…."

"What? Like Blaine or Franks? Because neither one is particularly unusual."

"Well, no, I guess not." Flynn sighed. "You told me at the hospital that your name was Christian. And you called me David."

"I was dreaming, I bet. They had me all looptastic." Christian? He was totally not pure and light.

Flynn frowned. "What does that mean?"

"Huh? That I was dreaming or high on pain meds?"

Flynn tilted his head. "I guess…. And because you knew about the guys in room 204, you used their names."

"What? What guys?" *Don't you go up there. You promised.*

"Jason told me about the research about Christian and David and how one of them was sick and the family wouldn't let the other one in the hospital, and he died, and the other one killed himself. Those guys."

"Yeah. Lots of folks die in the hospital, Flynn. That's what happens."

"Yeah, well, you started calling me David and making me promise not to go to room 204, and when I asked who you were, you said Christian. I guess there's been enough weird stuff going on that it freaked me out, and I thought you were being possessed by a ghost." Flynn looked pretty sheepish.

"That would be deeply fucked up."

"Yeah, no shit."

Blaine grinned. "I promise to warn you if I'm possessed if you swear to remove any weird bugs from my skin."

"It's a deal." Flynn held out his hand, and they shook. "This whole thing really is fucked up, isn't it? I don't know whether I want to wrap everything up and never go back there or really start looking into it."

"It's just coincidence, I bet. Seriously."

"Yeah? Probably. So we should go back next weekend and check out room 204, be sure there's nothing there to find."

"Next weekend?" No way. No fucking way. "If my shoulder is closed up all the way, huh?"

"God yeah, for sure. We can go the next weekend that you're up for it, eh?" Flynn touched his shoulder. "How's it feeling, anyway?"

"Numb. Weirdly numb." Dead was what he thought, but he wouldn't say it.

"Let me see." Flynn helped him get out of his T-shirt. "Wow, it's looking so much better than it was." Flynn touched gently. "And it isn't hot anymore."

"Good. It itched like fire before, you know?"

"I know. It looked awful too." Flynn leaned against him. "So is life with you always this exciting?"

"No. Not normally. I tend to work and hunt ghosts."

"Well, I have a theory that the ghost hunting is part of this craziness. I mean, maggots don't usually happen in live flesh. I think maybe the biter was a ghost."

The words maggot and flesh made Blaine want to gag. "I've heard of spectral bites, but... not this."

"Spectral bites?" Flynn asked, cuddling closer.

"Yeah, you know, random scratches, bites from nowhere?"

"Yeah, that sounds like what happened. Only it had a maggot stuck in its teeth or something." Flynn shook his head. "I don't know whether to be thrilled by having contact with the other side or freaked out that it hurt you. And I'm leaning toward freaked out. I was honestly worried about you."

"Yeah. Flynn, I have to tell you, if you say the word maggot one more time, I'm going to make you sleep in the car."

Flynn laughed, then stopped suddenly. "You're serious about that, aren't you?"

"Yes. No more m-word. Not until I have a good night's sleep and possibly a beer."

"I'll totally get us a couple of beers. If you're allowed to have them while you're taking meds."

Flynn wasn't going to be a stickler for the rules on this, was he?

"Thank you for running me to the hospital, man."

"I would have done it sooner if I'd realized what was happening. I figured we could just doctor it ourselves, though, you know?" Flynn got up and stretched. "Did you get a sheet of dos and don'ts with your meds?"

"Probably?" He'd just shoved everything in his bag.

Flynn snorted at him and started going through the bag with his meds. "Here we go." Flynn started reading.

"Tell me 'have a beer' is on there."

Flynn chuckled. "It doesn't say have a beer. But it doesn't say you're not allowed to have a beer either, so I'm going to assume we're good to go on the beer front."

"Works for me. Christ, I'm tired. Bone-deep."

"Why don't you head upstairs and pick a movie to watch or a show to binge on? I'll get us some beer and a snack and meet you there. We'll spend the afternoon hibernating."

"You sure?" Blaine was already up and moving.

"I'm sure. I think there's leftover pizza. The guys were hoping to see you last night, but lo, we were stuck in the hospital waiting for a doc to certify you officially bug-free." Flynn's voice faded away as he headed to the kitchen.

Whatever. Blaine didn't care. He just wanted to relax, rest.

He grabbed the remote on the way to the bed, groaning as he sat on the mattress. His own bed had never felt so good.

He patted his pillow, making sure there were no bugs, no eggs, nothing gross. Then he did the two extras and Flynn's too. Everything was clean, kosher. In fact he was pretty sure Mom had been here with clean bedding, not just pillowcases.

She was a trouper. So good to him.

Flynn arrived with a pizza box, a couple of beers, and a bunch of napkins, plus his bag of meds. "Most of these are 'take with food,' so…."

"Cool." Blaine stared at Flynn, blinked a couple of times, then sat up.

"You sure you need the beer?" Flynn asked, setting stuff down on the bedside table.

"I don't know, man. I just don't know anything."

"Well, it's here now. Just have a piece of pizza first." Flynn gave him a cold slice. "And when you're thirsty, have some beer. I bet you fall asleep before you're done with it anyway."

"I bet we both do. Have I said thank you for the help yet?"

"Yeah, but that doesn't mean you can't say it again." Flynn kissed him. "I'm just glad you're okay, babe."

"Me too. That was terrifying."

"It was. I say we forget about it for the afternoon and just eat and binge-watch *Penny Dreadful* or *True Blood.*"

"Okay. That sounds like one hell of a plan."

"I haven't seen either of them. You got a preference?" Flynn settled on the bed next to Blaine, sitting on the side of his good shoulder, and grabbed a slice of pizza.

"Don't care." He nibbled, hoping the food settled.

"Oh, I almost forgot." Flynn reached past him for the bag of pills and began doling them out. "You have to have food with all of them, and you can start on all of them at the same time. Man, they're really throwing the whole pharmacy at you, aren't they?"

"I guess, yeah. No one wants more ooky things coming out of me." Especially him.

"From your mouth to God's ears." Flynn squeezed his arm. "Okay. Here's this round of pills. Take them with water. I have a thing about washing meds down with booze."

"Yeah, that seems sorta… weird."

"Yeah, exactly." Flynn munched on his pizza, looking happy as a clam right where he was.

He leaned in, kissed Flynn's shoulder. "Sorry if I scared you.

"It's not your fault." Flynn nuzzled against his cheek.

"No? Cool." Because it felt a little like his fault.

"Of course not. Unless you put the bug in your shoulder."

He winced, his face twisting up.

"Yeah, I didn't think so."

"No. No, that was…." He shuddered, suddenly queasy.

Flynn rubbed his belly. "Don't think about it, okay? You need to keep those pills down."

"Yeah. Yeah, how did you know?"

"You all of a sudden went kind of green. Plus we were talking about the unmentionables. Just eat and watch the pretty vampire, okay?"

"Yes, boss." Eat. Watch the pretty vampire. He could do that.

"Oh, be careful. I could get used to being called the boss."

"I bet Jase would give you the job."

"You think so? I probably don't want it, eh?" Flynn rubbed their cheeks together.

"I'm not sure anyone does."

"Some people like being the boss, like the power. I'm not sure that ghost hunting encourages power-hungry guys."

"I think that ghosts would come for that, though, being power hungry."

"So you're saying we should go in there and start fighting over who gets to be the boss?"

"I'm saying that I want someone to talk to Jase once in a while."

"I don't get what you're trying to say," Flynn told him. "Sorry, I don't mean to be dense."

"The ghosts, honey. I just... I'm feeling a little wigged. Maybe someone else can be psychic."

"Oh! Duh! Sorry, I totally wasn't following you. I guess we do kind of put it all on your shoulders, don't we?" Flynn rubbed Blaine's belly again, the touch soothing, comforting.

"I'm sort of the only one who seems to do it, except for you."

"I'm a lightweight in that department compared to you. I mean, I do seem to see and feel more than the guys, but you have actual conversations with them and stuff. I could try to help more in that department if you want, though, babe."

"I just... I don't want to go back there right now." He never ever wanted Flynn to go back.

"Yeah, I don't blame you at all. So maybe the four of us will go while you're working the farm stand for your dad," Flynn suggested.

"No. No, let's just find another site for a weekend, huh? Something juicy and fun."

Flynn chuckled. "You've got a real hate on for that place, don't you? I suppose I can't blame you." Flynn touched the spot on his shoulder. "Do you think knowing about the couple who died got into your subconscious?"

"I guess? I didn't even know about them, really. I mean, lots of people died in that hospital."

"You knew their names, though." Flynn grabbed his beer and had a swig.

"I don't remember them." He didn't. He had a vague recollection of the story.

"Room 204."

"Stop it, of course you do. You said you were Christian, and you called me David."

Blaine didn't respond to that. He didn't remember it, he didn't want to remember it, and he didn't want to think about it.

"Room 204."

Jesus. Loud as anything. He looked at Flynn, but the man didn't look like he'd heard it at all.

Leave me alone.

"Room 204."

I'm serious.

Flynn was cuddled up against him, watching TV, obviously not hearing a thing going on. So obviously it was going on in his head.

God, was he going crazy? Was it the meds? The drugs? What?

"Room 204."

Jesus Christ. What was it going to take to shut that voice up?

"Room 204."

Stop it. I'll go look with a camera. I'll go, but I'll go by myself.

"Room 204."

"Room 204."

"Room 204."

"Room 204."

The words repeated over and over, getting louder each time.

"What?" Flynn asked.

"Huh?" He wasn't sure if he wanted Flynn to hear them or not.

"I thought you said something about a room."

"Just dozing, I think."

"Yeah? Okay." Flynn stroked his belly. "How're you feeling?"

"A little stoned still, I think." *Like I'm losing my fucking mind.*

"Well, considering I just gave you a whole bunch of meds, I doubt that's going to change anytime soon. Did you want me to turn the TV off? Would that make it easier to sleep?"

"No. No, I like that noise."

"Okay." Flynn settled again.

"Room 204."

The words started up again, only now they sounded angry, frustrated.

Flynn frowned and looked at him.

"Room 204!"

Eyes going wide, Flynn gasped. "That *wasn't* you."

"What wasn't me?" *Did you hear it too?*

"Room 204. I thought it was you saying it, but it didn't sound like your voice. And it wasn't even you saying it, because I heard it again, and your mouth wasn't moving!"

"I didn't say it," he whispered.

"Then who did? Because I'm not buying into shared hallucinations."

"How the hell should I know?"

"Well, it obviously has something to do with the hospital."

"Room 204. Room 204. Room 204."

There was an urgency to the voice now as it repeated the room number over and over again.

"I think we need to find out exactly who the guys who died there were and what happened to them." Flynn held on tight to him, looking around like he was trying to figure out where the voice was coming from.

"You have to promise me never ever to go to the hospital again, Flynn."

Flynn frowned at him as the phrase got louder, more strident. "I have a hunch maybe we need to go there to deal with this, Blaine."

"No. You can't."

"But why not, babe? The... whatever it is seems pretty adamant that that's exactly where we need to go. We should at least research it, dig deeper, even if we don't go there."

"Room 204!" It was a shout this time.

"Okay! We get it! Shut up already." Flynn shouted out the words, glaring at the air.

"I'll take care of it." Whatever it was. Whatever it needed. Blaine would deal with it.

Him. Alone.

"You're not facing this alone. You've got four guys more than ready to back you up. And if the others chicken out, you've still got me."

"You're suggesting...."

"I have no idea. I'm just saying that whatever's going on there, you don't have to face it alone. Whether we just need to research this and perform a ceremony of some sort, or whether we have to go back and face this at the hospital, you are not alone in this."

"Maybe I ought to be." Maybe he should. He knew, no question, that bringing Flynn to the second floor again would be... a huge mistake.

"No way. I'm not letting you do that. What if something happened to you?"

"Nothing will happen." He knew the words were false as soon as he said them.

Flynn shook his head. "I don't care what you say, I'm not risking you. Let's just hope it doesn't come to that. Maybe we'll get this figured out just by doing some research."

"Maybe. That would be cool, wouldn't it?"

"Yeah, it really would be. I'll get together with Jason and see what all you have, then dig deeper." Flynn chuckled. "And here I thought I'd be done doing research now that I've finished university."

"I thought that's what scientists did."

"Well, yeah, but into new things. We're going to be researching an old thing. Especially if we want to stay away from the hospital...."

"For a bit. Nothing will change. It's been what it is for years."

"Yeah, except now it's affecting you directly here at home." Flynn leaned up again and checked his shoulder. "It looks okay."

"Good. Good, that's what I want to hear." He didn't even want to suggest otherwise.

"Anyway. None of that is here or now. You're supposed to be resting. Getting better. So hush and watch the show already." Flynn settled back in against him, using him like a giant pillow.

Right on. Hush. Watch the show. Don't think.

Flynn stroked his belly, fingers warm and gentle. It felt good. Not even really sexual at all, more comforting.

"Glad you're here, man. For real."

"Yeah? I'm glad too, you know?" Flynn's eyes were bright and happy.

"Even with the grossness?" Blaine had to ask.

"Shit yeah. What's a little grossness between friends?" Flynn laughed. "I'd prefer less grossness in the future, but if you ever need someone to pull a bug out of you again, I am your man."

"At least you didn't say maggot." They started laughing together, the sound wild and a little hysterical, but real, intermingled. True.

Flynn settled back against him, warm and right.

Maybe he'd make it. Maybe it would all be all right.

Chapter Twelve

FLYNN sat with Jason in the living room, going through all the research they had already collected on room 204. They hadn't gone too deep into it; they hadn't needed to really for their purposes.

All they knew was the basics. Two gay guys in the eighties. One got sick with a brain tumor—Christian Singer—and his family had told the hospital not to let David Swans in under any circumstances. When Christian died, David killed himself. In the hospital room. Room 204.

A shiver went down Flynn's spine.

There wasn't much—a couple of newspaper articles, a mention of David Swans's sister, two obituaries that listed totally separate families.

"Is this everything you found on the internet, or did you just do the basics?" Flynn needed to know where to start looking.

"There's not much. It was pre-internet. Daisy Swans, the sister listed, is living in Australia now. The Singer family just disappeared. I mean, I bet they had friends, but…." Jason shrugged.

"Well, let's put their names in a search together and see what we can find. We can hit the library up next for the newspapers."

"Sure." Jason sighed. "You really think they're active, these two? I mean, you've got the violent death downstairs…."

"Yeah, but…." He didn't want to give Blaine up, so he shrugged in turn. "I have a feeling."

"Cool. Do you think it has to do with the bite? That thing's prodigious."

"Yeah, I really think it does." He cleared his throat. "Okay, so this is going to sound a little out there, but let me talk it through. I think he was bitten by a ghost. Flies don't lay eggs in live flesh, only dead flesh. So how did the maggot get inside him? It was in the thing that bit him's teeth." Yeah, okay, it sounded a little out there. But then the whole thing was out there.

"Okay, so yeah. Out there, but worse than that— really fucking scary."

"I know. But I can't see any other explanation. I mean, I didn't bite him, and something definitely happened to him in the ER. You were there. You saw him."

"Yeah. Yeah, so, what? What do we do?"

"I don't know. Learn everything about Christian, David, and room 204. See how it's connected. If it's connected."

"But if it is? What do we do then? I mean, silver and sage?"

Flynn nodded. "To start with. We'll look up everything we can find on putting them to rest."

"Well, that's better than letting them eat us. I mean, seriously, what if there's an attack? If we can't get it on camera…."

Flynn nodded. Blaine would be happy if he wasn't the only one not wanting to go back. But Flynn hated just leaving it. Something was there, going on, and he wanted to figure it out. Help, if it was a situation where they could. "We definitely need to be careful. No unnecessary risks."

"Rock on. By the way, are you looking for a day job, man? There's an opening at my call center."

"Doing what exactly?" His frugality meant he had savings still. He'd been paying rent with it, but he preferred not to dig into it too deep if he could help it. As long as he had a roof over his head and food enough, he liked to save that kind of thing for a rainy day.

"Answering phone calls, helping people out. There's a lot of calming angry customers down for the most part."

"I'm not sure I'm the calming-angry-customers-down kind of guy. I appreciate the offer, though. Can I let you know?" He supposed the hours would be pretty flexible, which was always a good thing when coupled with the ghost hunting.

"Sure. I like to hit my friends up first, you know? Sometimes the hours suck, but it's a job."

"I hear you. I guess we aren't getting any cash flow soon on the actual ghost hunting, eh?"

"Not yet. I'm working at it. The last bit of footage with Blaine acting like a psycho is pretty cool, and so is the story of the bite. I'm thinking about taking him out there to 'get bit' on-screen."

"Not without me." He looked Jason in the eye. "Promise me you won't do anything like that, just the two of you—that you'll bring me along."

"Sure. I'll need someone to run the camera, right?"

"Right." He wasn't sure it was a good idea to fake something like that, but he figured they could revisit it later. For now, he just wanted the guarantee that Jason wouldn't take Blaine to the hospital without him.

Jason stretched and went back to his laptop, slowly running videos from their visits. "Where's Blaine? He should be done at the stall by now, huh?"

Flynn glanced at his watch. "Huh. Yeah, he should. Maybe he went to see his folks." He grabbed his phone and texted, *where u at?*

bringing food. Mom made stew

yum!

"He's on his way with stew from his mom." Flynn's stomach growled, and he realized he'd skipped lunch.

"Rock on! I hope she sends cornbread too." Jason grinned at Flynn. "We used to love that when we were all in school. Coming out here for food."

"Like you don't still love it." Blaine's mom was a fantastic cook.

"God, my favorite is chicken parm day."

"That sounds great. I haven't had that yet. I have to admit, there's nothing like home cooking from someone's mom."

"Oh dude. My mom is the queen of takeout—Chinese, pizza, Greek, curry."

Flynn laughed, shook his head, but he had to wonder a little bit—had Jason and Blaine been lovers? Darnell? Any of them?

"So, an all-gay ghost-hunting team. Did that just happen, or was it deliberate?" He tried to keep his tone casual.

"It was six of one, half dozen of another. We were all friends because we're gay. It was me and Blaine who started talking about the ghost hunting."

"Were you ever together?" Keep it smooth. Keep it casual. He glanced over, trying not to look too interested.

"Together? We said we were dating in high school, shared a couple of hand jobs, and then decided we didn't do it for each other."

Flynn chuckled, more relieved than he was willing to say. He was about to make some glib joke about it being awkward to have work relationships anyway, but then he realized he was in one, so it would be better not to make the joke. Of course, he didn't consider what he and Blaine had as a work thing.

"Seriously, it's cool if you two are a thing. Blaine's a decent guy. A little down on his luck, but aren't we all?"

"Some would say that's what we get for being ghost hunters." Flynn grinned. "I happen to think the world is waiting for five gay guys hunting ghosts, and we just need the right circumstances and bam, we'll be bigger than the Village People."

"Oh dude." Jason's eyes lit up. "Do you think we can get Blaine to wear the leather-daddy outfit?"

"You absolutely cannot." Blaine was at the screen door. "Let me in, you freaks."

Flynn popped up off the floor, cackling like a loon as he went to open the door for Blaine. "You would look really hot, man."

"Shut up. What the hell are you two talking about?"

"How we could be the Village People of ghost hunting." There was nothing abnormal about that, right?

"The Village People… wow. Stew?"

Flynn laughed and grabbed the pot from Blaine. "Are those homemade rolls too? Your mom is a treasure."

"She's feeling better. Seriously. It's so fucking cool."

"Excellent. How about you?" Jase asked. "How's the shoulder?"

Flynn peered at Blaine's shoulder, but he couldn't pull the shirt or sweater back with his hands full of the pot of stew. "You need me to doctor it?"

"I will, yeah, but after. Jase, grab bowls."

They all helped, dishing up the stew and gathering utensils, putting out the bread and butter.

"I love that you have butter instead of margarine. It always tastes better, especially if the bread—rolls—are homemade." Flynn grabbed glasses and pulled the milk out of the fridge.

"Oh, do not get Mom started on the horrors of oleo, huh?"

"No margarine talk with your mom. Got it." He gave Blaine a wink, sat, and dug into his stew. Damn— rich and thick and peppery and stunning, it tasted like heaven in a bowl.

"God, this is good. How do you get to become a good cook like this? Because I'm an okay cook, but this is amazing."

"I think it's a mom thing," Blaine said. "I mean, maybe your mom skipped those lessons, Jase."

"She totally must have. I mean, you've seen her actually burn boiling water."

"Seriously?" Flynn asked, laughing when Jase nodded.

"It caught fire, man! *Fire*."

He cackled, and Blaine chuckled along with him. "Seriously."

Blaine nodded. "Yep. Actual fire. We put it out with the extinguisher."

"That's…." Flynn just stared. "Wow."

He looked up and met Blaine's eyes, and they both laughed. Flynn really loved Blaine's laughter, and he knew he wanted to spend a lot of time hearing it.

"So we're talking about going back to the hospital and filming you getting bit, man. Thoughts?" Jason asked.

"Is that kosher?"

"Are we going to ever break into a deal if we don't do better?"

Flynn sighed. "I'm not against going back to the hospital. I'm just not sure about faking the bite, man. Anyone finds out we did that and we lose all credibility."

"You don't think all those guys with shows don't go back and film pickups and stuff for their narrative?"

Flynn didn't know. He just wasn't sure it was something they should start.

"We can at least film the bite now, right? Show what happened."

Blaine nodded once, just a dip of his chin. "That I can do."

"Yeah, I'm down with that too." Flynn could get behind the truth.

"You guys are two peas in a pod. Seriously."

Flynn grinned over at Blaine. "We're peas, apparently."

"Podlike peas." Blaine began to chuckle.

Flynn's lips twitched. "Wait, wouldn't that make us aliens? Shouldn't we be more like ghostlike things?"

"Ghost peas?" Jason pursed his lips. "I'm not sure. Ghost Peas sounds like a band name."

"Maybe that's what we should call the team. You know, to sell us. Blaine the Brain and the Ghost Peas investigate yet another haunted building." Flynn was cracking his own shit up.

"Oh my God. We need a website—Brain and the Ghost Peas!" Jason was howling.

Flynn gave Blaine a private smile, reaching out and touching his hand, and Blaine twined their fingers together.

Oh God, were they basking? It felt like they were. He rather liked it. Hell, he loved the idea that he had someone here, someone to bask with. Someone not in the hospital with bugs in his shoulder.

He squeezed Blaine's hand. "Hey, Pea."

"Do you want to be Pea Two or Pod?"

"I'll be the Pod to your Pea any day."

Jason snorted. "You two are gross."

"Hey, you're the one who said we were two peas in a pod. We're just playing along." Goofing about.

"Yeah, and I'm wicked jealous, just FYI…."

"Oh. Um, sorry." Flynn felt bad now, like they'd been flaunting it in Jason's face.

Blaine smirked. "Don't be. He rubs my face in his boyfriends whenever I'm single."

"Oho. You do, do you, Jason?" Flynn threw a corner of his bread at Jason. "Butthead."

"Well… okay. Yeah. I totally have."

All three of them laughed and went back to their food.

Flynn sopped up the last of his stew with his bread. "We had just started looking into Christian and David. The guys associated with room 204."

"Did you find anything?" Blaine looked worried.

"Not yet. We hadn't really gotten very far into it."

"Well, I know it's a sad fucking story, right?"

"Yeah. Christian was sick, and his family wouldn't let his lover visit. He finally got in to see him and it was too late, so he killed himself. Kinda Romeo and Juliet, eh?"

"Yeah. Creepy." Blaine shivered, arms wrapping around himself.

Flynn put his hand on Blaine's shoulder and squeezed. "It is. And if they need help getting to rest, we'll do that for them, okay?"

"Yeah." Blaine didn't sound so sure.

"What's wrong, babe? This whole thing has had you on edge big-time."

"I just…. There's something wrong." Blaine shook his head, then stood and started cleaning up the dishes, shoulders hunched.

Flynn got up and went over to his lover. He didn't even bother with the pretext of bringing more dishes. "So talk to me. Tell me what's wrong. I can't help if you won't talk to me."

"I just think we should let it go. Leave them alone."

"But…." He wasn't sure he was going to be able to just forget everything.

"Room 204."

Shit. "I'm not sure it's going to leave us alone."

"It will. They have to."

Jason stood, frowned. "Did you two hear that?"

"Room 204."

Flynn whipped his head around to Jason. "You heard it too?" Okay. This was happening. That was all three of them now, not just him and Blaine.

"I'm fucking calling the rest of the guys. Someone turn on the tape recorders."

"Room 204."

"Room 204."

"Room 204."

It repeated over and over again, and Flynn went for the equipment stored in the dining room, looking for the recorders.

"It won't matter. They won't pick it up."

"They'll pick us up, though, and we're hearing it." Jason grabbed his phone, and punched his finger at the screen.

Flynn brought the recorders into the kitchen and turned them on. The room number continued to be repeated, sometimes a whisper, sometimes louder, and honestly, it was beginning to freak him out.

"You think we should go back and check out room 204?" Surely that would put an end to this.

"No!" Blaine looked weird for a second, wild.

Flynn went up to him. "Babe. You have to tell me what's going on. And don't tell me it's nothing. Every time room 204 comes up, you freak the hell out."

"You can't go in there, David!"

David. He hadn't imagined it this time for sure. Blaine had called him David. Which was the name of one of the couple. The guy who'd killed himself.

"Why not, Christian?" Flynn asked, playing along for a moment to see if he could actually get more out of Blaine.

"You know why. You know. You know they'll kill you. You know that. He'll kill you."

"They? He? Who? Who will kill me?"

"You know." Suddenly Blaine's bright blue eyes turned dark, almost brown. Like they had physically changed color. Weird.

"No. No, I don't know. You have to tell me." Oh God. This was insane. It was fucking creepy.

"Blaine? Blaine, what the fuck is wrong with you?" Jason stormed over, grabbed Blaine's arm, and shook him hard.

"Don't!" Flynn pushed Jason away. "We have to figure out what's going on." Then he turned his attention back to Blaine. "Come on, Christian. You have to tell me. You have to. Come on, now. *Tell me.*"

Blaine looked at him, blinked. "Tell you what?"

Flynn sighed, seeing nobody but *Blaine* there. "You're back, huh? For a minute there I swear you were Christian, and you were actually going to tell me what the deal with room 204 is."

Blaine frowned. "Stop it."

Jason stared. "It's true, man. Seriously."

Flynn nodded. "You called me David. You responded to Christian. You were saying that he or they were going to kill me, and that's why you didn't want me to go to room 204." It made Blaine wince every time Flynn spoke about that room.

"Just stop it." Blaine shook his head. "Stop saying the room number."

"Then tell me what's got you so freaked out!"

"Shit, why shouldn't he be freaked? We heard someone who wasn't there saying things here in the barn!" Jason wasn't helping.

"I agree, Jason, but I'd like to know *what* he knows."

"I don't know anything. I didn't do anything, man."

Flynn sighed. "I don't like this. I don't like it at all. It's like this thing gets a hold of you, and there's something there but it won't let you tell."

"Darnell is on the way," Jason noted. "Will has to finish his shift, but he'll be here in a few hours."

"We'll get everything set up and see if we can't figure out what the fuck is going on." Flynn started pacing, trying to work everything out.

Blaine began to pace too, striding the length of the island in the kitchen. Every now and then they met up and did the "you go, no you go first" dance.

"So what should we do? More research, or are you not telling us stuff, Blaine?"

Blaine looked at him, cheeks going bright pink. "Excuse me?"

"I don't know if you only know it when Christian takes you over or if you're just scared to tell me, but there's stuff that you aren't telling me. Stuff about room 204."

Jason stared at them both like they were crazy.

"What? What stuff? What the fuck are you talking about?"

"Christian and David and room 204!" Flynn looked into Blaine's eyes. "Tell me about room 204."

Blaine ripped away from him and stormed upstairs. A moment later the bedroom door slammed shut.

"Goddammit." Flynn followed him and stood outside the door. "Blaine! Blaine, we can't just ignore this! It isn't going away!"

"Leave me the fuck alone!"

"Don't be like this, Blaine. Please? Come on. We need to deal with this."

He heard something hit the door, and then he heard sobs. He turned the door handle, cursing when it wouldn't budge. Blaine had locked it.

Flynn banged on the door. "Come on, Blaine. Let me in. You can't keep shutting me out." Something bad was going to happen.

Maybe something bad was happening now.

Jason's voice came from downstairs. "Blaine? Flynn? Do you guys need me up there?"

"Let me see if I can get him to let me in." Flynn banged on the door again. "Blaine? Let me in or we're breaking the door down." Maybe he was appealing to the wrong person. What if Christian had hold of him again? What if Blaine was hurt?

"This is my room, dammit!"

"Blaine! I mean it. We need you with us, not hiding up here alone where anything could happen to you."

The door flew open, and Flynn noticed immediately that Blaine's shoulder was bleeding again, a slowly expanding red spot on his shirt.

"Jesus. Did you hit your shoulder on something? Sit. Let me look at it."

"I'm not going to be accused of withholding information about some fucking assholes who died before I was even born!"

"I don't think you're doing it on purpose, babe. I think there's something here. Something... I don't know. Let me look. Let me see." He went over and tugged at Blaine's shirt.

Jesus. The wound was torn open again. Fuck.

"Were you scratching at it?" Flynn carefully removed Blaine's shirt, then called downstairs, "Jason? Bring me the first aid kit, please."

"Is he hurt again? Christ. Come downstairs."

Flynn rolled his eyes and looked at Blaine's shoulder more closely. It was a bloody mess, like someone had been scratching at it for ages. "Did you do this? Were you scratching?"

"When? Between slamming the door and walking across the room?"

"I don't know! It's all open and bloody like someone's been tearing at it, and if it wasn't you...." He met Blaine's eyes. "This is moving into fucking scary, love."

"I know." Blaine looked exhausted, frightened, more than a little lost.

Flynn hugged Blaine tight, careful not to touch the bloody mess. "Don't shut me out, okay? We need to face this together. And obviously we can't ignore it." Something wanted them to go to room 204, and it was getting vicious about it.

"You can't go there. You can't. It's a terrible idea."

"I get that. I don't know why you think that, but I get that you feel really strongly about it. And I'm more than willing to try work-arounds. But it really seems like all this scary shit isn't going to stop unless we do." And Flynn wanted as much information as he could get. He wanted Blaine to tell him what he knew. Or what he thought he knew.

"I don't understand what the hell is going on. I don't get it, but I know that you can't go, that it's dangerous. I *know*." Blaine grabbed him, squeezed him. "You just have to believe in me."

"I do believe in you. That's why I'm willing to try to do as much as we can here. See if we can't get rid of whatever it is that's... doing this shit."

"I don't even know what to do."

"Stick together, hmm?" He hugged Blaine tight. "Come on. Let's go down and get you doctored and start researching."

"Darnell's pulling up now, guys," Jason called.

"The troops are all rallying around. We're going to be okay. We've got friends, people who are in our corner."

"I don't even know what—"

"Shh. Shh, please. Let's just stay calm. Focused, huh? We're going to wire up the barn and figure out what the hell is going on here. We have the know-how." Flynn kissed Blaine good and hard, smashing their lips together.

Blaine's eyes went wide, and then he wrapped one arm around Flynn's waist. Flynn let himself get lost in the kiss, in Blaine's taste.

"Guys. Guys, seriously? Now?" Jason sounded close by and… shocked.

Groaning, Flynn broke off the kiss, cutting a glance back at Jason, who was now standing in the bedroom doorway. "It's never a bad thing to remember what you're fighting for."

Jason made a kissy face. "Man, if I'd known Flynn was gonna be so hot, I would have made a play for him."

"Fuck off, Jase."

Heat climbed Flynn's cheeks. "He's in the room."

"And he's a little stud," Blaine said.

Flynn's mouth dropped open, and he turned to stare at Blaine. Then he smiled. "You think I'm a stud?"

"Duh." The response was gratifyingly immediate.

He kissed Blaine again. "Thank you."

"Freaks. God. So jealous." Jason made Flynn chuckle.

"Okay. Let's get downstairs and doctor your shoulder and then set up to catch whatever it is that's haunting us and send it back to hell." They trooped down, Flynn being careful Blaine didn't trip.

"What's going on?" Darnell came bursting through the door, four pizza boxes in hand. He delivered for a living and got to keep any mismade pies. "Blaine's back is bad again, and something is haunting the barn. It keeps saying 'room 204' over and over again. I heard it." Jason sounded pretty excited.

"No shit? Did you catch it on tape?"

"We set them up, but hadn't caught anything as of last night," Flynn noted.

"Let's check it out." Jason grinned and grabbed half the pizza boxes.

"After I doctor Blaine's shoulder," Flynn added.

"I'm fine."

"Did you know they were together, man?" Jason asked Darnell, looking smug as they set the pizzas down.

"Who, Flynn and Blaine? How long?"

Jason looked at him and Blaine, and Flynn shrugged. "A few days."

"Before or after Monday?" Darnell asked.

"What does…?"

Blaine rolled his eyes. "There's a bet."

Darnell nodded. "Will owes me ten bucks if it was before Monday."

"Seriously?"

"Totally. Ten bucks is ten bucks."

Flynn shook his head. "That's not classy at all."

Darnell snorted. "We hunt ghosts, and you two live in a barn. We aren't exactly the height of class here. Besides, it's not like either of us was wrong—you guys are doing the deed."

Blaine snorted, and suddenly, blessedly, they were all laughing, howling with it.

"Will totally owes you ten bucks," Flynn admitted, and they all burst into laughter again.

"And here I was told there was an emergency," Will said, coming in with the rest of their equipment. "Not *Laugh-In*."

"You owe me a tenner, man. Did you see Blaine's shoulder?"

"Oh." Will turned green. "No. No way. No looking. I don't do blood."

"Well then, look away. I have to doctor it." Flynn sat Blaine down and began patting at the blood. "You swear you didn't scratch at it? Because it's not pus-y, but it's been opened up."

"I didn't touch it. Just close it back up. We have more butterfly bandages."

"I know, but someone—" He looked at the others. "—or something did." They needed to get this figured out before anything worse happened to Blaine.

"For real?" Will asked. "I mean, you guys aren't just fucking with us?"

Jason shook his head. "No way. I heard it too."

"Heard what?" Will asked, looking at each of them in turn.

"Room 204," Jason said. "And it wasn't any of us."

"Yeah." Flynn shivered. "Over and over again. And I think that the bug in Blaine's shoulder came from a ghost bite too."

Will looked at them like they were crazy. "Blaine? Are you with them on this?"

"I don't know. Ghosts don't.... I mean, I just don't know."

"Then how do you explain it?" Flynn asked. "I'd be happy for alternatives, believe me. But if this is a prank or something, well, then you guys must have pissed someone off pretty good. Have you?" He looked at each of the guys in turn.

"A prank? How do you make this a prank?" Will and Darnell looked confused as hell, while Jason seemed ramped up.

"Well, that's my best alternative to it being real. What's yours?" Ghost or not, this was happening, and it was physically hurting Blaine and freaking them all out on top of that.

Will looked at Darnell, who shrugged. "I got nothing, man."

"Let's get the equipment set up and see what we get." Flynn left Blaine's T-shirt off, the white of the Band-Aids stark against his skin.

"Like I said before, I want us to shoot Blaine's wound too," Jason added. "Just to have a record."

"Yeah," Flynn agreed. "Then we can show any changes that happen there too. Like how it now looks like someone scratched his skin open." Flynn chewed on his lower lip, nerves eating at him.

"I didn't do it, Flynn." Blaine looked so serious.

"I believe you, babe. That's what makes this so worrying. Something *did*. And if it can do that, who knows what else? I really don't want to find out it can harm you even more than it has already." He took Blaine's hand and squeezed. "We are going to figure this out. That's what we do, right?"

"I work on a farm and try to talk to ghosts on camera."

"We actually hunt for the ghosts, though, right? We want proof that there's specters haunting the places we go to? So we're going to find evidence here, if there's any to be found." Though again, he was hard-pressed for any other reason why they were all hearing voices and Blaine had developed a bite that had turned into a bug's burrow, and was now a sore that seemed to be getting bigger on its own.

"So let's lay it all out for the camera." Flynn nodded at Will, who hoisted the camera on his shoulder, the little red light blinking on to indicate it was taping.

"You want to explain what we're doing here, Blaine? Just like you would if we were out on a case."

"Sure." Blaine grabbed a T-shirt from the pile in the laundry basket in the hall and slipped it on before looking into the lens. "Hey, guys. This is my house—and four days ago we noticed a little bite on my shoulder."

Flynn tried not to make a face because he knew Blaine didn't like thinking about the maggot that had been inside him.

When Blaine didn't explain further, though, he figured he should, as he was the one who'd had the best view of the thing. "It was a pretty big bite, actually. Looked like a human bite, and it had broken the skin. It was warm to the touch, and an area about the size of the bottom of a beer can was quite red. So we decided to doctor it by pouring some hydrogen peroxide on it— make sure it was cleaned out."

Blaine continued. "I pushed on it and... man, there were bugs in it. Seriously, bugs."

Flynn didn't bother to correct Blaine that it had been one worm. That had been awful enough. "So we went to the hospital, and they checked it and pumped him full of antibiotics and sent him home. Now nobody has touched the wound except to change the Band-Aids, but now it looks like someone has been tearing at Blaine's skin."

Will moved in with the camera, and Jason pulled back the edges of the butterfly bandages to show the sore.

"Dude.... That's nasty."

"Don't say that!"

Flynn shook his head. "It actually looks clean. I mean, it's covering a bigger area, but it's not nasty. Why don't you tell them about room 204," Flynn suggested to get Blaine's mind off his shoulder.

"In 1984, Christian Singer died in room 204 from a brain tumor, and the family kept his lover, David Swans, from saying goodbye. By the time David got in to see Christian, it was too late."

"Assholes," muttered Darnell, and the others added their approval.

"It gets worse, though, doesn't it?" Flynn prompted.

Blaine nodded. "David died in the hospital. In that room. Standing next to his lover's body."

"How did he die?" Flynn asked. Blaine was still being recalcitrant about sharing information on room 204, and Flynn was going to prod him until he'd divulged everything he knew. At this point, they all needed to be on the same page.

Blaine shook his head, and then they heard, *"Room 204!"*

"Did you hear that?" Flynn asked, looking into the camera. "None of us said that."

"Room 204."

"Blaine, I think you need to tell us what happened to David. How did he die?"

"How should I know? You guys looked it up."

Jason went to the laptop. "I think he committed suicide, yeah?"

"Room 204."

"Are you hearing this?" Will asked.

"I'm hearing it. In case you're not picking it up at home, we're hearing a voice saying room 204 over and over again." And the more Blaine resisted, the louder it seemed to get.

"Yeah, he shot himself in the head."

"Room 204."

Blaine dropped his head into his hands. "It hurts."

"We're trying to figure out what's here with us, and why it's hurting Blaine, and how to get rid of it." Flynn was worried the only way they were going to succeed was to go back to the hospital, but Blaine was resisting that big-time.

"Dude. Flynn, grab a Kleenex. His nose is bleeding."

"Shit!"

Flynn grabbed some tissues and handed them to Blaine. "The more you resist talking about room 204, the more you wind up hurting." He knew Blaine didn't want to hear it, but it was what was happening. He had observational data on it now. "Don't stop taping, Will."

"I won't. I'm getting it all."

"Me too." Darnell was taping from a different angle.

Flynn stayed with Blaine, made sure his nose stopped bleeding. He summarized for the camera while he was doing it. "So we have the medical death of one man and the suicide of his lover. All of this happened in room 204."

"Room 204."

"And someone or something seems to want us to investigate. I have a hunch it's not going to stop unless we go to the hospital and check out the actual room 204."

Blaine shook his head. "It's a bad idea."

"Room 204."

"Room 204."

"Room 204!"

It was shouted this time, and Flynn frowned, shook his head. "I'm not sure we have a choice. Whatever is here is hurting you, Blaine. We need to get this dealt with."

Darnell's face was gray, eyes huge. "I don't like this, guys."

"No, none of us do." Flynn hated it, in fact. He wished it was happening to him and not Blaine. He still wouldn't have been happy about it, but then at least Blaine would be safe. "But it came to us. Or followed us home or something."

"Do we have footage of that room, man? From before?" Darnell looked to Jason, eyebrows arched.

Jason shook his head. "No. I don't think we spent any time in there aside from some prelim stuff. Man, we should have checked the place out better."

"No, we were up there. Me and Blaine, what, a year ago? You remember, man? Long time ago," Darnell said.

Flynn looked to Blaine. "You have more to tell us about 204? Come on, babe, not talking is killing you."

"We went in, filmed. It was just another room."

"But you're trying to keep me away from that room. You keep telling me how dangerous it is and asking me to stay away from it. How would you know if you were hardly in there and it's just another room?"

"It's just a bad idea, you know?" Blaine looked so serious.

"I believe you, babe. But look around us—look at yourself. Not doing anything isn't an option anymore."

"Let's look up the footage. I'll call Jill and ask." Jason grabbed his phone.

"We could always move out," Flynn suggested. "Pack up and go across the country. I'm sure they've got haunted buildings on the West Coast." It wasn't really a suggestion, more of a tease, but the voice suddenly started screaming "Room 204!" over and over.

Blaine clapped his hands over his ears, and Darnell just headed for the door.

"Stop that!" he shouted. "We're trying to figure it out, so just stop!"

"This is fucked up. We're taking the stuff and heading to my place. Now." Jason started grabbing laptops and camera cases.

Flynn was torn between wanting to get to the bottom of this and wanting to get away from it. He took one look at Blaine, whose nose had started bleeding again, and nodded. "Okay. Yeah. Let's do it."

"They've been there since the '80s. Let's go. We'll call Blaine's folks from my place."

Flynn put his hand on Blaine's thigh. "You want me to throw some of your stuff into a bag, babe?" He was pretty sure Blaine hadn't even heard him.

"Grab his medical shit, and I'll grab the pizzas."

Flynn dashed upstairs and threw a change of clothes for both of them into a bag, along with the stuff for Blaine's shoulder and their Kindles. He swore he could still hear "Room 204" echoing through the place, but he was putting that down to his imagination.

All the what-ifs ran through his head, maddening as a bunch of bees buzzing in his skin.

The biggest one was what if something happened to Blaine. What if this injured him worse than he already was?

Flynn shook himself and joined the guys out at Will's van, letting Blaine lock the barn. Jase and Darnell had their own cars there in the driveway. "Who are you two riding with?" Jase asked.

"Will has more room in the van, I guess," Flynn replied. "Here, Blaine. You take the front seat." He opened the door for Blaine, who was already looking less pained.

Blaine climbed in without an argument and settled with his eyes closed.

Flynn hated what this was doing to Blaine. This was way more serious than any of them had signed on for. They were supposed to look for and document ghosts, not find themselves in the middle of a horror movie.

"This is some crazy shit. Do you think you were the catalyst, Flynn?" Will swung up into the seat and then started the van as Flynn climbed in.

"Me?" Of course it had started when he'd joined the team. They'd been to the hospital without him plenty of times already. "Maybe. I don't know."

"Hey, if you are, it's not like you're at fault, huh?"

"Sure, that's easy to say." He chewed his lower lip. "Blaine doesn't want me anywhere near room 204. I mean, like, violently doesn't want it. But every time he says that or refuses to talk about stuff, that damn voice starts up again."

"We'll figure it out, all five of us." Will grinned at him, winked. "Right, Blaine?"

Blaine shook his head. "You have to stay away from room 204. It's not safe."

This again. Flynn sighed. "I don't know. Not going seems pretty dangerous too."

Blaine turned and pinned him with a sure look. "It's important."

"Explain to me how not going to room 204 is more important than going so we can get rid of whatever it is that's haunting our asses. I won't go if you don't want me to, Blaine—but you can't just say 'it's dangerous.' You have to tell me why I can't go."

"I don't know! I just *know*."

Will gave him a look in the rearview mirror, but Flynn ignored him in favor of leaning in and grabbing Blaine's arm, giving it a squeeze. "Okay, babe. Okay. I will promise you that I will be really careful, and that I won't go to room 204 without letting you know." He wasn't going to promise not to go at all, because what if that was the only way to save Blaine? If that was the case, then dammit, he was doing it.

"Thank you. Thank you, honey." Blaine relaxed, went boneless.

Christ, he didn't understand what was going on. Not at all. It wouldn't have been so bad—oh, it still would have grated; he was into finding things out and exposing them after all—but it was clearly hurting Blaine, and that meant he couldn't just ignore it.

He put his head back and closed his eyes as Will drove them to Jase's place.

At least the damn voice screaming room 204 at them had finally quieted.

Chapter Thirteen

THEY ate the pizza first, and there might have been more than a couple of beers before anyone wanted to talk.

Hell, Blaine wasn't all that sure he wanted to talk regardless.

Flynn touched his good arm, startling him out of his thoughts. "Let me check your shoulder, okay?"

"Yeah. Yeah, okay. I'm sorry about all this, guys. Really."

Jason snorted. "How's it your fault?"

"Yeah, exactly. You're the one being hurt by it the most." Flynn lifted his shirt and touched him lightly. "It's not any worse. Might even be a little better."

"We're here. Ghosts don't haunt piece-of-shit apartment buildings," Darnell drawled.

Flynn chuckled softly as he settled next to Blaine. "I imagine they haunt what they need to haunt."

"So, what do we know?" Will asked.

Jason shrugged. "There's footage of when Will and Blaine did the room last year. Jill's sending the file names so Flynn can look them up. I know that the brain-tumor guy had a family that didn't let the lover in and that he got in after... an aunt smuggled him in, I think? A brother? Something. Then he died from an apparent suicide."

Blaine shook his head. It wasn't a suicide. He knew that, but he couldn't know that, right? That was crazy. The man was out of his mind with grief and pulled a Romeo and Juliet.

"Not a suicide?" Flynn asked, eyes wide. "Someone killed him?"

"What?" Jason looked as confused as fuck. "Who said that?"

"Blaine—he shook his head no when you said the lover died from suicide."

"Did I?" Had he? Really?

"Well, yeah. Didn't you? Am I going crazy now?"

"No. No, I just... it was instinctual, you know? Like it didn't feel right."

Will held up one hand. "Wait. Let me set up the static cameras in case something happens, okay?"

Flynn nodded jerkily. "Yeah, yeah. Sure. Sorry I misinterpreted, babe. But what makes you think it wasn't suicide? And who would have killed him?"

"Why would you bring a gun to a hospital to see your lover?"

Darnell nodded. "That's what I was wondering."

Flynn's eyes went wide. "Oh man. You're right. Somebody killed him, and they fobbed it off as a suicide. No wonder his spirit is unquiet. We need to make this right."

"Guys! No more words until cameras are rolling!" Will's voice was disgusted. "You are the worse wannabe celebrities ever."

That broke the tension that had begun to build again, and they all burst out laughing.

Blaine grabbed the last piece of pizza, then offered half to Flynn. Huh. Must be love.

"Thanks, man." Flynn scarfed it down, then chased it with the last few mouthfuls of his beer. "I didn't realize how hungry I was."

Yeah, they'd been too busy being fucking haunted.

"Okay, we're rolling. Now you can talk to your heart's content." Will came back and sat. "Did you get the file names for the film yet, Jase?"

"Not yet. Blaine, Flynn, why don't you both go back to talking about the new discovery about David's supposed suicide?"

"Well, I don't know that it's a discovery. I just feel— strongly feel—that it wasn't a suicide." Blaine believed it, and every time he said the words, he believed it more.

"Yeah, we were talking about it, and we couldn't help but wonder why someone would take a gun to the hospital to visit their sick loved one. I mean, he wasn't planning to kill himself, was he? He was trying to see his lover and didn't know Christian had died." Flynn looked like he was pondering things.

"Right," Blaine agreed. "And was there anything to say that David was violent? What did he do for a living? Did he have a criminal record? What about Christian?" Away from the barn and the shouting voice, Blaine could think again, and his brain was crowded with questions.

"Looks like it's time for some old-fashioned research."
Flynn grinned. "I know this one has an unhappy ending, but
I do like a good mystery."

Jason nodded, fingers tip-tapping away at his
keyboard. "There's got to be more information here
than we thought there would be."

"Well, you never looked that hard to begin with,
right?" Flynn asked. "I'm not saying you did too little,
just that you didn't need to look into it that deep, right?"

"I only had the basics, until you asked about it
today."

"Okay, then. I guess we should start digging.
Figure out what exactly happened with Christian and
David, look into their lives."

"Yeah. Yeah, okay," Blaine agreed. "Flynn, you
and Darnell can hunt up the film from that night, and
I'll work with Will on the footage we just shot."

"And I'll keep digging on the net," Jase added.

"Rock on." For the first time in a while, Blaine felt
like he could breathe. Really breathe.

"It's always good when a plan comes together,"
Flynn noted.

"It's something, all right." Blaine grinned, though.
"Let's see if we can hear anything from the barn footage."

Flynn stopped what he was doing to listen in.

They were there, looks of true panic on their faces,
but the ghostly voice was nonexistent.

"How is that possible?" Flynn asked. "We were all
there. We all heard it. It was damn loud at some points!"

"I don't know. I don't…." Blaine stopped and
tilted his head. "What the fuck was that?"

"What?" Flynn crowded him and hit Rewind.

"Look." Blaine was reflected in the mirror above
the fireplace. The glass was shaking, shimmering, and

he swore there was someone behind him, draped over his shoulders.

"Oh my God!" Flynn looked behind him like he expected the guy to still be there. "Shit. Guys, you have to see this."

Blaine's skin crawled a little, though. He wasn't sure he wanted to see it again.

They backed it up and played it frame by frame, and it was totally there.

"That's fucking creepy, man." Darnell shook his head. "I know we're goddamn ghost hunters, but that's not cool."

"It looks like it's sitting on your shoulders, Blaine."

"No, it looks like it's whispering in your ear."

"No, it looks like it's trying to merge into him." Flynn rubbed Blaine's back with one hand, like he was trying to reassure himself that the thing wasn't still there.

"It's not cool, whatever it is." Blaine shook his head, swallowed hard, and then stood. He didn't want to see that.

"This is amazing." Jase sounded excited. "We've never had such clear film of an actual entity!"

"I just wish it wasn't at Blaine's expense," murmured Flynn, shivering. "God."

"Is it biting on him?" Will whispered.

Flynn shrugged. "Something bit him. And the bite looked more human than buggish. And then something tore it all open again earlier today. So you tell me."

"Ew. Let's not talk about that, huh?" Blaine was going to gag.

"Ixnay on the aggotmay," Flynn told the others.

They went back to their separate corners to fulfill their various tasks.

Jason sat up suddenly. "Fucking weird. It says here they died on May 12, 1984. Isn't that the day you were born, Blaine?"

"It's my birthday too," Flynn said quietly.

Blaine stared at Flynn. "What?" No way.

"Swear to God. Down to the year."

"Well, Christian died around noon, and they heard the shot around two for David," Jason shared.

Flynn shivered. "I was born in the afternoon."

"I don't know. Don't ask me what time I was born. I *was* born at that fucking hospital!"

"Oh my God!" Flynn sat there with his mouth hanging open.

"Jesus. Jesus." Darnell looked gobsmacked. "Are we saying…?"

"I don't know what we're saying." Jase started making notes. "But it's a huge coincidence that you were both born the same day as the couple from room 204 died. And that when you both showed up at the hospital together… things started happening."

"It's all like a setup. It has to be."

"By who?" Flynn asked. "I mean, who would do that to us? Why? It doesn't make any sense."

"I'm as big a fan of a good conspiracy theory as the next guy, but I've got to admit that Flynn raises a good point. Who would do it and why?" Darnell scratched his head and shrugged. "There's nothing on the tape of you and Will going through the room on the initial run-through. I mean, *nothing*. This all started when Flynn showed up. Hey—have you got any enemies, man? Maybe this is because of you and not Blaine."

Blaine looked to Flynn. "Ex-boyfriends? Jealous scientists?"

Flynn shook his head. "I was always the breakee—not that there were many. As for scientists...." Flynn shrugged. "I'm not exactly in a popular field, you know?"

"True that." Jason frowned. "So let's assume that it is supernatural. What do the ghosts want?"

"For us to go to room 204." Flynn held out his hands. "What? Don't look at me—that's what I'm getting from it."

"You can't go there." Blaine was sure of that. Knew it would be a terrible idea.

"You keep saying that." Flynn sat back. "But I'm not letting this hang on to you. We don't know if it's doing more than just putting bugs in you and ripping open your skin. Maybe it's zapping your energy too, taking years from you. I don't know what's real and what's not, but you're being hurt. That's real."

"You two just keep thrashing over the same shit," Will said.

"What if the three of us went and did a live feed?" Jase asked.

"Which three—you, me, and Will?" Blaine asked.

"No, I meant Darnell, Will, and me," Jase answered. "You said you didn't want Flynn there. I'm guessing he doesn't want you there either."

Flynn didn't hesitate for even a second. "You got that right."

"That's fair, I guess. Do we have any information about them? Anything new?"

Jason shrugged. "David was a schoolteacher, and Christian was an artist. David had a sister here in town who was killed by a bus about five years after David died."

"What about Christian's family?" Flynn asked. "The ones who wouldn't let David see him."

"There was a mom and dad, a brother, an aunt. Superconservative types. Dad was a minister."

"Oh man. That had to be rough on Christian. Poor guy." Will shook his head. "We should go do this now, yeah? Get it done."

"It's already late, guys. You could go tomorrow. In the daylight."

Flynn nodded vigorously at Blaine's suggestion. "I think that's a great idea. I know we need to solve this, but daylight sounds way safer than going at night."

"That makes sense." Darnell didn't look all that eager to go. "Let's research tonight."

"Sure. And maybe Blaine and I should go with you. Maybe we should sit out in the van outside. In case you guys need backup," Flynn suggested.

"We'll discuss it tomorrow," Blaine said. "We're all going to pretend like we're not total dipshits and research tonight."

"Damn, I was kind of going for total dipshit," Flynn teased him, eyes twinkling.

"You and me both. I wanted another beer and a *Stargate* marathon."

"Oh, I like it." Flynn nodded. "What do you say, guys, is it a plan?"

Jase threw up his hands. "What the hell."

Thank God. Blaine couldn't go back there. Not yet. Not now.

Tomorrow he'd find another excuse.

Chapter Fourteen

FLYNN and Blaine sat hunched over the laptop in the van, watching the camera feed as the guys went up the stairs on their way to room 204.

"You think they'll be okay?" Flynn asked. He hoped so. He didn't think it was going to help, but he had a hunch they were going to be okay. Flynn thought he and Blaine were ultimately going to have to go up there to deal with whatever this was. All signs pointed that way.

Blaine held his hand, squeezing it tight. He squeezed right back, his eyes glued to the screen.

The guys made it up the stairs and moved along the corridor, slowly. It was funny how it looked like nighttime in the corridor with no windows to let in the afternoon sun. Funny but not funny, really.

He swallowed as they stopped in front of a door and focused the camera on the number on it: 204.

"They shouldn't go in," Blaine whispered.

"Babe, they have to. We've got to deal with this. We do." Flynn was nervous too, and if it was just a matter of getting establishing shots or checking out something weird going on with the hospital, he'd be totally down with calling the whole thing off. But something had followed Blaine home, for fuck's sake, and was hurting him. It had to be done.

They needed to put this to rest somehow, give David and Christian peace. Flynn was convinced that was the only way he and Blaine were going to find their own peace, now that they'd become connected to the story. He didn't want to examine how closely, given they were both born the same day that David and Christian had died. Looking at that too closely was just plain spooky.

There were a lot of things Flynn was discovering he didn't want to be curious about.

"There they go," he murmured as the guys opened the door to 204 and went in, the room looking fucking creepy lit only by a few cracks in the blinds over the windows and their flashlights.

"Open the blinds, man," Will said, and Jason nodded.

"We're in room 204, looking for evidence of the couple who died in this room in the 1980s—David and Christian." Jason walked over to one of the windows, grabbed the cord to the blinds, and tugged.

"Be careful!" Blaine said, shocking the hell out of Flynn as the entire set of blinds came down, crashing to the floor in a poof of dust.

Flynn gasped. "How did you know?"

"Because I've done it. Like eighty fucking times."

Flynn shook his head. "No, you told me you were only in there the once to check it out. You guys haven't even been here eighty times."

"I meant the blinds in old places."

"Oh." Flynn laughed and nudged their shoulders together. "Sorry. I'm seeing ghosts around every corner, it seems."

"It's understandable, I think." Blaine leaned against him and spoke into his mike. "You okay, Jase?"

"Nothing hurt but my pride, man. Possibly my shirt."

Flynn chuckled and tapped on his earpiece to turn it on. "I bet both can be fixed with a little duct tape."

"Yeah, yeah. Can you two see clearly?"

To be honest, there wasn't all that much to see: a sink, wires, a single IV stand in the corner, and dust. Lots of dust.

"Yeah, we can see just fine. Unless you're seeing something that we're not." Flynn shook his head. Why did he keep thinking that the only way this was going to get fixed was if he and Blaine went in together?

"Dust. Dirt. There's not a lot in here."

"Run some EVPs, man. Talk to them. See if they'll answer." Blaine grinned a little bit, just the barest smile. "It's your chance to be the lead."

"Fuck you, man." Jase threw him the finger.

Flynn snorted. "You're on camera, man."

"Yeah, yeah. Edit it out."

"I totally will." Darnell snorted. "Come on. Let's do this. It's creepy in here."

"Any EMF readings?"

Darnell held the machine up to Will's camera. "Some. Not enough to be significant, but too many to disregard them out of hand."

"But there's no cold spots. And nothing on the monitors to indicate anyone's here."

"Someone's there," Flynn said. "I can feel it."

"Someone's always there," Blaine noted.

A bang sounded in his earphone, and the guys in the room started looking around, the camera swinging wildly, making him nauseated for a second.

"Was that a shot? You hear that, Blaine? That sounded like a shot." It took everything he had not to bound off his seat and run in there.

"I guess? I don't know. Guys? Guys, is everyone okay?"

"Yeah, yeah. We're good." Jase shook his head. "That was definitely a shot, and it sounded like it came from in here. None of the readings changed, though. It's like they're resisting the machines or something."

"Do you see anything?" Flynn asked. "Try the EVPs now. See if Christian or David will talk to you."

God, his heart was racing. He kept hold of Blaine's hand, gripping it like it was a lifeline. Maybe it was.

He heard Jase asking Christian to talk to him. Then David, Jase trying to encourage any specters to make contact. Flynn didn't hear anything, but when he looked at Blaine, his lover shrugged.

"Lots of times we don't until we play it back. You know that."

"I know. Things have just been so strong with this room, I expect it to work, you know?" He thought they wanted him and Blaine here, so why clam up? Well, because they hadn't gone in; the others had. "Maybe they're waiting for us to show up."

"You can't go in there."

"To save you from the ghost chomping you to bits, yes I can." He was more afraid of Blaine getting hurt than of any ghost in room 204.

The sound came again, louder this time, almost like it was in the van with them.

Flynn looked at Blaine. "Babe. We aren't going to be able to solve this from here. We need to go in and figure it out. Don't you think these guys deserve peace? *Don't you?*"

"You don't understand." Blaine's shoulders were hunched, his head lowered between them.

"You're right, I don't. I get that something terrible happened there—and that was before we knew someone was murdered—but if we're going to shake loose of it, we have to go." He was going to say it again and again until either the ghosts were gone or Blaine finally agreed with him.

"No, David. You don't understand." Blaine swung around, and suddenly it wasn't Flynn's lover there. It was a stranger. A dark-eyed man.

It stunned Flynn so badly he didn't even see the movement as something came down on his head, knocking him out cold.

Chapter Fifteen

FLYNN'S head hurt, like really, and he groaned as he reached for the back of his skull. He squinted, the sun almost painfully bright until he shaded his eyes.

He was in the van, half sitting, half lying in the back seat. The laptop was on its side on the floor in front of him. He squinted harder to make out the picture. It was the stairs of the hospital—the guys were obviously on their way down after... after being in room 204.

"Blaine?" He looked around, but Blaine wasn't in the van with him. "What?" He couldn't see Blaine anywhere, not on the grounds, not on the steps to the doors of the hospital, nowhere.

The guys burst out of the doors a second or two later and headed right for him.

"Flynn! Blaine! You guys all right?"

He blinked, looking at them as they pulled open the side panel door.

"What happened? You guys all of a sudden stopped communicating."

"Yeah, we thought something had happened."

"Hey, where's Blaine?" Darnell asked.

"I... I don't know." They'd been watching the guys on the monitor, and then all of a sudden…. He put his hand on his head and groaned again. Someone had hit him. Hard.

"Jesus. Jesus, Will, grab me a towel or something. Where's Blaine?" Darnell asked.

"I don't know! He didn't go up to room 204?" Flynn blinked, trying to clear his mind.

Will passed a towel to Jase, who grabbed Flynn's hand and lifted it to put the cloth between his head and his hand. "You're bleeding like a son of a bitch."

"Oh."

"Looks like you got clocked pretty good."

Well, that explained the splitting headache and the pain where he was pressing the towel against his scalp.

"Who did this to you, man?" Darnell asked.

"I don't know." He remembered the look on…. He hesitated to say Blaine's face, because it sure as hell hadn't looked like Blaine. "Something's really wrong with Blaine."

"We need to get you to the hospital, Flynn." Jason looked worried as fuck. "Darnell, can you see Blaine anywhere out there?"

"Give me five to look; then we'll take him."

Flynn shook his head and regretted it immediately. "No, I'm okay. We need to find Blaine first. He can't have gotten that far on foot, right?"

"We can look for him on the road, maybe? I don't like this, Flynn."

"No, I don't either. I don't…. Guys, I don't think he's in his right mind. After we heard the shots, he started freaking out. He called me David, and the last thing I remember was him yelling at me, and his eyes…." He shivered. "It wasn't Blaine in there. We *have* to find him."

"Okay. Okay, uh, Darnell? Will? Ideas?"

"I'm trying to call him," Will said. "I don't want to get his parents involved until we have to."

"Are any of you on the same network as he is? Most of them have that find-my-friends app," Flynn suggested. He was totally going to set up software on all their phones that let them track each other.

"Uh…. That's a thing?"

"I'll go outside, see if I can see… I don't know, anything?" Darnell grinned at him, rolled his eyes. "I'll channel my inner Boy Scout." He walked off briskly, and Flynn spared a moment to appreciate his new friends.

"Pass me my phone." Flynn leaned back against the seat, his head pounding harder as he moved.

"I really want to take you to the hospital, man. That looks bad." Jason peered at his skull. "I don't understand. Blaine did this to you?"

"No. It was someone else in Blaine's body."

"That's it, time to get him to the hospital," Will said. "Let's go."

"No," Flynn insisted. "Something's got hold of Blaine, and we need to find him before something awful happens to him. I mean, he hasn't got a car or anything. Where the hell is he?"

"Well, I—shit. Shit! Call his phone again, Will." Jason hit the side of the van, cheeks a dark red, and

Flynn could see it—how much Jason cared about all of them, how scared their self-appointed leader was.

"It'll be okay, man. We're going to find him. We're going to figure this out." He wasn't sure he believed it—the pit of worry in his belly was hard and ugly—but he needed someone to believe it, and he could pretend that was him for now. He was hurting, but he didn't think having a meltdown was going to help that. Besides, he didn't have meltdowns. He just didn't. And if he was on the verge of having one, well, it would just have to wait.

"What...? Okay, so let's assume it was the Dave guy in Blaine," Jason started, and Flynn shook his head.

"No. No, it's Christian. No question."

"How can you be so sure?" Jase asked.

"Because he called me David. And it wasn't the first time either." God, had he just not been paying enough attention? No, no. He had been. He'd called Blaine on it a couple of times. This wasn't his fault. Right?

"Okay, so, Christian. He was local, right? Where would he go?"

"Oh, that's good. Look up his home address. See if you can find anything." Why hadn't he thought of that? Maybe because he'd been beaned over the head and the man he was falling in love with was possessed by the ghost of one half of a dead couple.

"Right. His home address. The family's address. Maybe his work or his lover's work."

"See what you can find, and we'll try the closest place first," Flynn suggested.

"Yeah, that makes sense."

Will's fingers were already flying over his phone. "I got nothing on the home address, but the school is still open and downtown, and the family owned a dairy farm just... I mean, just about four miles from here."

"Four miles? Blaine could totally walk that. Hell, how long has it been since you lost contact with us?"

Jase checked his watch. "Uh. Maybe twenty minutes."

"If he was running, he could totally almost be there by now." Flynn sat up and dropped the towel from his head. Hopefully it wasn't bleeding anymore. He put on his seat belt. "Let's go."

"Well, let's get Darnell first. He'd be pissed if we left him."

"I suppose we should. Phone him and tell him to get back here pronto." Flynn had a bad feeling at the back of his mind, and it wasn't from the bash he'd taken. Something was wrong.

"I'm on it," Jason called. Will typed in an address, and Flynn focused on not puking.

He took a few deep breaths and tried not to think of Blaine with those dark eyes that totally belonged to someone else. God, this was fucked up big-time.

"Come on, come on. We need to get going."

"Darnell was on the other side of the hospital. He found Blaine's phone, shattered."

"Shit." Flynn's stomach jumped into his throat, worry eating hard at him. "Tell Darnell to hurry. We need to get moving before anything happens to him."

Why would Blaine break his phone? Why on earth?

Because it wasn't Blaine anymore.

Flynn pushed that thought aside along with the lump of worry. He breathed a sigh of relief as Darnell came back, running.

"What's the plan, guys?" Darnell closed the door, plopped in the seat. "Calling the cops?"

"What? No! What would we tell them anyway? 'Excuse me, but our friend is possessed by the ghost of this guy who died in the hospital we're investigating and we can't find him'?" Flynn shook his head emphatically. "We're going to check out Christian's family's farm. It's only about four miles from here."

"Rock on. I was just thinking, what if the knock on the head confused you and Blaine's been taken?"

That stopped him short, and they all looked at him as he considered it.

"I suppose it's a possibility, and if things hadn't already been weird and creepy, I'd highly entertain it as our number-one possibility. How about we go check out this dairy farm, and if he's not there, we can reconsider the calling-the-cops option?"

"Sounds fair. A little scary, but fair."

"This whole fucking thing is scary," Flynn noted. Maybe he was supposed to be all macho and shit, but he was really worried about Blaine and couldn't put up a front.

"You think?" Jason rolled his eyes. "I've been doing this shit with Blaine for years, and we've never ever seen anything like this."

"I guess you just needed all the right elements in place, eh? You are taping, right? If we can get anything on tape, this is the type of thing that gets you your own show. Maybe even some grant money to make it. New equipment and shit. I mean, as long as we're getting some of the stuff recorded. The other day we had bupkes despite the fact that there was tons in person." Flynn knew he was babbling, but if he didn't he was going to scream at Will for driving so slowly, even though he knew it was because the road was bad for the first half mile or so and Will was just being careful.

"Yeah. Yeah, you have a point. We're recording everything."

"Good. Good. Because Blaine is going to be pissed if he finds out we weren't." Flynn refused to contemplate them not finding Blaine.

Will hooted. "Blaine is going to be pissed if he's possessed. The man gets grumpy when he's distracted."

"I think being possessed comes with a get-out-of-jail-free card." It was a poor joke, but Flynn was trying. He really was, but he didn't like how this whole thing was shaking out.

Darnell nodded. "Totally. We'll solve this a la Scooby Doo and gang."

"Uh, dude," Jason pointed out. "Scooby only had real-life bad guys. We have a ghost."

"Ghosts!" Will added.

"Ruh-roh?" said Flynn.

They all cracked up, and Flynn actually had to snap his mouth shut to stop. He was far too close to hysteria.

Darnell reached out, squeezed his hand. "It's cool, man. We'll find him."

"Yeah, I know we will." He just hoped Blaine was in his right mind when they did.

They stopped in front of a dilapidated old farmhouse with a rusted old Ford pickup parked in the drive. The paint was peeling, and ivy almost engulfed the whole place.

Flynn frowned. "You think anyone lives here?"

"It looks like someone's here, for sure." Will stared. "Should we go knock?"

"Yeah. It's not like Blaine would have left a vehicle in the driveway—he was on foot."

They all piled out of the van and approached the front door, Darnell and Will filming. Flynn looked at Jase, who nodded, and so he'd lifted his hand to knock when he heard a voice.

"You killed him! You bastard!"

"You're insane. I don't know what you're talking about!"

"Oh fuck." Deciding to forego knocking, Flynn tried the door, nearly falling into the place when it proved to be open. Then he did go in, calling out for his lover. "Blaine!"

"You stood there and shot him in the head while he cried over my dead body, you fuck! Jerry, I watched you!"

Blaine was standing there making the accusations, but it didn't sound like Blaine, and Flynn felt something cold run down his back.

What the actual fuck?

"Who the fuck are you guys? That's it! I'm calling the cops!" The man had lank, greasy hair and a thin face with a pinched expression. He was dressed in sweats and a flannel jacket, which fit in with the surroundings just about perfectly.

"Call them!" Blaine roared. "You shot David Swans, my lover, your own brother's lover, while he was holding my hand! I saw you!"

Flynn's eyes went wide. "You're Christian's brother. You kept them apart when Christian was dying!"

The guy turned and ran, heading for the back of the house, and Blaine took off after him. Flynn had no choice but to follow.

"Blaine! Stop! Uh, Christian! Come on, he's not worth it. We'll call the cops." He was worried Blaine—or Christian or whatever the fuck had possessed him—was going to do something stupid. Better to let the cops sort this out. There was no statute of limitations on murder, right?

And as far as he knew, possession was not a defense.

Blaine moved fast, almost a blur, and Flynn knew Christian was pushing him. He caught up with them in the bedroom, Christian's brother standing on one side of the double bed, Blaine standing on the other.

Flynn grabbed Blaine's arm. "Come on, man. Let me call the cops, and they can deal with this." He had his phone in his hand to prove it wasn't an empty offer.

"Get the fuck out of my house!" Christian's brother was red-faced with anger, but there was a hint of uncertainty in his expression as well.

"It was our house, Greenie! It was ours. I smoked my first joint with you out in one of the empty stalls. We used to build forts in the back. It's not yours!"

The guy—Greenie, and what the hell was that short for?—lost some of his color, and the look in his eyes was more than a little freaked out.

"I don't know you, you freak! Shut the fuck up and get the fuck out of my fucking house!"

"Hey, now." Flynn let go of Blaine's arm and took a couple of slow steps, figuring he could go around the bed, more or less get between Blaine and this Greenie guy. "Why don't we all just take a few breaths?"

"Blaine? Flynn? You guys okay?"

"Go outside, Jase!"

Fuck yes, the last thing they needed was all five of them in here with this guy already on the defensive like this. "Blaine and I have it, Jase. We'll be out soon. Right, Blaine? How about we go out and take a breath or two and let Greenie here do the same thing?"

"You killed him. You shot him in the head, Jerry. You shot him in the head because why? He wanted to tell me goodbye?"

"He was sick!"

"I was sick! I had a fucking brain tumor! Dave could have gone on to live a long life." That wasn't Blaine's voice.

"And what? He could corrupt someone else?"

Fucking shit. This Jerry guy had actually killed David. And hadn't even denied it. Was in fact trying to justify it.

"You killed your brother's lover after your brother was dead?" Flynn asked. And Jerry thought there was something wrong with Christian and David for who they loved? Christ.

"Fuck you. Get the fuck out of my house. Fucking fags, digging up dirt on good families."

"You did!" Flynn was outraged now too that this man had actually killed someone just for being gay. "How can you live with yourself?"

"How can I...? That motherfucker made my brother sick and damned him to an eternity in hell!"

"I had fucking cancer. Cancer!"

"The AIDS. No one wanted to tell us, but I know that was it!"

"It was brain cancer, you asshole," Flynn hissed. "And he didn't get that from his lover. That's not how cancer works. The guy just wanted to see the man he loved before he died, and you took that away from him, and then you took his life too. God, you make me sick." Like, physically ill. He knew a part of it was the whole my-lover-is-possessed thing, but a part of it was this asshole too.

Blaine—Christian—stabbed a finger at Jerry. "And you killed him. You killed him for loving me."

"Shut up!"

"You held the gun to his head, and you shot him!" Blaine's scream rang out, so much louder than anything Flynn had ever heard come from a human throat.

"Shut up! Shut up! You aren't him! You can't know!"

Jerry made to lunge across the bed at Blaine, and Flynn couldn't have that. He ran the rest of the way around the bed to stop him and came up against the hard circle of a gun's muzzle, pushed right against his chest.

Flynn gasped and froze, his eyes going wide, and he slowly raised his hands. "Okay. Okay. Okay. Let's all just take a breath." Oh God, he was going to die.

"You fucking queers, looking into things. It's done. It's all done now. It's over. Suicide. He shot himself in the head and—"

"No." That was the not-Blaine voice. "He was devastated, but he had his whole life ahead of him. He was young."

The gun pressed harder into Flynn's chest, and he swallowed. "Uh, Blaine. Or Christian." Whoever was in control right now. "He's got a gun...." Just in case he hadn't noticed.

"Christian is dead!" Jerry screamed, and suddenly, impossibly, Blaine slammed himself between them, the report of the shot loud, stunning Flynn.

He waited for the pain to hit him, but it didn't, and he grabbed his chest, but it was fine—no hole, no bullet, nothing.

Blaine stood there, staring blankly, and something... separated from him. Like a mask peeling off.

Flynn moved to Blaine's side, nearly tripping over what proved to be Jerry on the floor, in a puddle of blood.

Oh God. "Blaine! Blaine, come on. We have to get out of here. We have to call the police."

"You killed him, Jerry. He was a good man. He was my good man."

Oh fuck. Fuck. "Leave Blaine alone!" he shouted, his arm going around Blaine's shoulders.

The form—because it didn't look like a man, it didn't look like a man at all, but this red, fuzzy mist— advanced on Jerry, beginning to cover him.

"Oh fuck. Blaine, I think we should get out of here. I don't know what the fuck is going on, but that thing was *in* you. *In* you." He tugged on Blaine, needing to get his lover moving.

Blaine stared at the form. "It's okay to be angry," he whispered. "Thank you for keeping Flynn safe."

"Babe. Come on. Before it decides you're its permanent ride." He tugged harder, trying to get Blaine moving.

They needed to call the police.

Will was standing in the bedroom doorway, camera in hand, filming. "He shot himself. Guys, he shot himself."

He hadn't even realized the guys had ignored him and followed them back here. "What?"

"He just shot himself. I have it on tape."

Flynn looked back down and shook his head. That hadn't been what happened, had it?

"I don't...." What the hell? "Let me see."

"Let's get out of here first. Wait for the police outside," Jase suggested.

Blaine was simply standing there, staring. Flynn nodded and grabbed Blaine's hand, tugged him along.

"Come on, Blaine. Seriously. You did what you were supposed to, right? You brought Christian here."

He kept dragging Blaine with him until they were out. Then he put Blaine into the van, sitting him down. "Breathe, babe. It's okay. I'm pretty sure it's over now."

Blaine just sat there, blinking slowly.

"Blaine? Man? You with us?" He took Blaine's face in his hands and looked into his lover's eyes. "Blaine? Come on, man."

Those blue eyes looked vacant, empty. Like Blaine was sound asleep.

"Blaine. Man, you're scaring me now." Had carrying Christian done something to his mind? He slapped Blaine's cheeks lightly, just enough to wake someone from a deep sleep, and Blaine took a deep, deep breath, blinked at him, stared.

"Flynn."

Oh thank God. "Blaine. Are you okay, man? You gave me quite the scare."

"I—where are we? What's going on? Why are you bleeding?"

"Seriously? I'm bleeding because you walloped me over the head."

"What? I did not!" Blaine looked at Flynn like he was the one who had lost his mind. "I wouldn't…. Why are the police coming?"

"Because Christian Singer's brother was shot."

"Killed himself," Jase interrupted.

"Maybe you'd better let us take a look at that film before the cops show up so we know what the fuck our story is here."

"Well, the sirens are coming, so you'd better hurry up." Darnell was so not helping.

"I know what's on camera. The dude pulled a gun out, Blaine grabbed you, and he shot himself."

"What do you remember, Blaine?" Flynn asked, snatching the camera and hitting the playback.

"Sitting in the parking lot at the hospital and hearing the shots."

"Seriously? That's the last thing you remember?" That was fucked up. He turned his attention to the playback. It was just like Jase had said. Jerry had a gun out, Blaine pushed Flynn out of the way, and Jerry turned the gun on himself. Flynn shivered, no sign of

Christian's ghost. At all. "Christian was there, guys. I swear to you. He was there."

"Don't tell the cops that. Why were we here?"

"Asking questions about the hospital," Jason said. "That's the truth."

Flynn nodded. "Yeah, yeah. Looking into the two guys from room 204. The camera proves we didn't do anything but talk to him and get out of his way when the gun came out." He was entirely freaked out and pissed off too that they didn't have any proof.

Still, this kept him and Blaine out of jail, mostly Blaine. Right. Right. It was a good thing. It was. He was just freaking out a little.

"I'm going to see if we can get you to a hospital for your head, Flynn," Jase said. "When the cops ask about that?"

"I fell out of the van." Flynn was freaked out enough about everything that it would be believable.

"Fair enough. Okay, guys, game faces on. You ready?"

Flynn looked at Blaine, who looked back, and they nodded together. Yeah, they had this.

They had to.

Chapter Sixteen

THEY fell into bed without so much as speaking to each other. Flynn had ended up with his head shaved and a bunch of butterfly bandages. Blaine's shoulder had been repacked. Mom and Dad were livid and scared, and the guys just wanted to go home.

They slept through the night and most of the next day, and it was getting dark when Blaine managed to get his eyes open.

Caffeine.

God, he needed caffeine.

As soon as he moved, Flynn grabbed hold of him and muttered something indistinct.

"Mmm. Hey. You want a Coke?" He held Flynn's hand a second, hoping he wasn't scared of Blaine now.

Flynn clung to him. "I'll come with you."

"'Kay. We might have eggs or something." He felt like he'd been out of touch for eons.

Flynn got up and rubbed his face. "Yeah, I guess I'm hungry. I'm still feeling kind of stunned over the whole thing."

"I guess I owe you a thousand apologies, don't I? I'm so sorry."

"For what?" Flynn looked honestly confused.

"Hitting you with the camera? Getting weird? I don't know."

"Hey, you were possessed at the time. I think you're forgiven." Flynn laughed, the sound short. "Now there's something you don't expect to find yourself saying."

"No. No, that's true." He squeezed Flynn's hand. "So, are we still... friends?" Lovers? Something?

"More than friends, right?"

He let out a relieved breath. "Yes. Right. Oh good. I was.... Well, I was worried."

"That would make me a pretty lousy guy. Because you either were haunted by a ghost, which makes it not your fault, or you weren't, which means you saved my life when you pushed me out of the way of that gun."

"Do you think it was Christian? The thing on me?" He thought it was over. The heaviness on his shoulders, on his soul, it was gone.

"I know it was. He was talking through you. It was creepy. It sure as hell didn't sound like you." Flynn shivered. "You looked like you had brown eyes, honey. Seriously."

"Why did it happen, do you think? And why didn't it happen to you, I wonder."

"Well, I have a bit of a theory, only you might not like it."

"Then let's go get that Coke and we'll talk about it."

"Okay. Works for me." Flynn got out of the bed and pulled on a pair of sweats. When they were both dressed, they headed downstairs.

Flynn kept one hand on him, and it was comforting, warm, grounding. They were so new that Blaine simply didn't know what the best thing to do was.

They got their Cokes and a box of crackers, then went to the living room to sit on the couch together.

"So. My theory. I think we're connected to Christian and David. I mean, they died the same day we were born. You were even born in the same hospital. For all I know, so was I. I hate to use the word reincarnation, but…." Flynn shrugged. "And you've got a stronger connection to apparitions than I do, so it was easier for Christian to get a hold of you."

"I don't know, but I know that I was scared for you, going up to that room." Blaine didn't even want to say the number.

"Yeah, you were pretty insistent that I not do it." Flynn tilted his head. "What about now? You think it would be safe to go back. See if Christian's still there or if we helped him… move on?"

"I don't know, but I don't feel that… horror."

"I kind of feel like we should go. Make sure they've moved on. I think we deserve to know."

"Maybe not tonight."

Flynn laughed softly and leaned against him. "No, babe. Not tonight. Probably not even tomorrow. Maybe next weekend. Maybe. I feel like we need the closure, you know?"

"Yes. Right now we need… peace." Blaine needed to reconnect.

"Peace?" Flynn smiled at him, the look sweet, almost coy. "I was hoping for something a little more, uh, energetic."

"With your head?" He reached out, stroked Flynn's scalp.

"We don't have to swing from the rafters or anything…."

"You're awful!" Blaine laughed, though, charmed.

"Uh-huh. You're going to do it with me, though, right?" Flynn gave him a hopeful look.

"Maybe a hand job. Maybe. If it doesn't hurt you. I've hurt you enough."

Flynn grabbed him and kissed him. "Stop that. It wasn't you. And I think Christian was trying to keep me safe, believe it or not."

"Do you? I didn't want to hurt you. I know that. I… I have a connection with you."

"Yeah. Me too." Flynn stroked his belly. "I like how your skin feels."

"Do you?" That was comforting, warm and sweet.

"I do. Especially your belly and the bits below."

The touches continued, sweet and gentle, and Blaine's eyes crossed with the electricity Flynn was building. Flynn leaned in again, pressing their lips together. Warm and soft, it felt as good as the stroking along his abs.

"We're supposed to be gentle and good and not…." But he wanted to.

"Not what?" Flynn asked, cuddling closer.

"Being sexy."

"Who says we're not supposed to be sexy?" Flynn asked, eyes close, watching him.

"Probably the doctors. You have a head injury, love."

"It doesn't hurt that much anymore. We can be gentle, eh?"

"We can. I can. I promise never to hurt you again."

"Shh. It wasn't really you—you haven't hurt me." Flynn begged a kiss.

Still, Blaine had guilt. Flynn would wear the marks of this for the rest of his life.

"Blaine. Kiss me, man."

He loved that Flynn still wanted him to. Loved it. He leaned in, brushed their lips together.

"That wasn't a kiss, it was a tease," Flynn complained, eyes twinkling at him.

"No? Let me try again." He offered Flynn another kiss.

Flynn was smiling as their lips met, and he opened his mouth, inviting Blaine in. He hummed and slipped his tongue in, tasting Flynn carefully. Flynn closed his lips around Blaine's tongue and sucked. He wrapped his hands around Flynn's hips and drew him closer. Flynn hummed for him, the sound all pleasure.

Every little sound made Blaine more confident, made his need that much greater. Flynn kept touching his belly, rubbing and tracing his muscles, which jerked and tightened, clenching. God. He wanted.

"I can feel how hot you are, and I want to touch you." Flynn tugged at Blaine's jeans, pulling open the top button.

"I want… I want you, honey."

"Yes. God, yes." Flynn got Blaine's zipper down, pushed his hand into Blaine's jeans, and wrapped it around his erection.

He hadn't thought he was going to be hard, that he was going to need. He did, though, and Flynn worked him, increasing his desire.

"Love how you feel in my hand," Flynn murmured.

"Feels good." Blaine didn't have any other words.

"Really good." Flynn pinched the tip of his cock, a quick, sharp little squeeze.

Blaine's eyes crossed. "Yes!"

Lord.

Flynn stroked quickly, moving his hand up and down like he was trying to start a fire.

"Gonna make me come, Flynn," Blaine warned.

"Uh-huh. That's why I'm doing it." Flynn met his eyes, leaned in and kissed him again, hand still working.

"Never met anyone like you. That I just… knew."

"I know. Pretty cool, huh?" Flynn rubbed the tip of his cock.

"Uh. Uh-huh. Very. God. More." How had he been reduced to this already?

Flynn squeezed his cock tight, then stroked up and down along his length. "More. You're so pretty."

"When…. After…. I want to suck you."

"Okay." That was it. Just okay.

Blaine laughed, even if the sound was a little strangled. Flynn swallowed his sounds with another kiss, cupping his balls as well, rolling them.

He cried out, so very close, and he spread wider, acting like a total slut. Flynn jostled his balls and stroked him harder, the actions undeniable, and Blaine's belly clenched as he let go, let Flynn have him.

Flynn moaned when Blaine came. "God, I do love how you smell."

He blinked, eyes on the way Flynn stroked him, up and down, nice and gentle now, rubbing his seed into his shaft, making the skin shine.

"Better, eh?" Flynn asked, finally letting go.

"Uhn." That was an answer, right?

Flynn laughed and carefully tucked him back into his pants, got him done back up with a little pat to his package. "Good one."

"Uh-huh." He got that. He slid down onto the floor, pulling at Flynn's sweats. "My turn."

"Oh goodie." Flynn raised his ass so Blaine could get Flynn's sweats off. Once he'd disposed of them, Flynn spread his legs, giving Blaine room between them.

"Eager." Blaine liked that. More than that, he liked how Flynn was hard and begging for him, leaking at the tip.

"You're going to suck me off—of course I'm eager. A dead man would be eager for that mouth."

"Flattery." He loved it.

"Just take the compliment," Flynn told him, laughing softly.

"I can do that." He ran his cheek along Flynn's cock.

Moaning, Flynn spread his legs wider, and Blaine took advantage, leaning in and rubbing the soft sac with his chin.

"Is this a blow job or a rub job?" Flynn asked, then started giggling.

Blaine blew a raspberry at the base of Flynn's cock, teasing.

The laughter increased. Flynn closed his legs slightly, cradling Blaine, who snuggled right in, hands sliding up the outside of Flynn's thighs.

"Feels good. Want more," Flynn told him, dropping a hand to Blaine's head and carding his fingers through Blaine's hair.

Blaine dragged his tongue up along Flynn's shaft, making sure not to miss an inch. Flynn's moan was louder this time, and his legs spread open again, Flynn bucking slightly to push closer. Blaine let Flynn in, let the tip of his hard cock rub against the roof of Blaine's mouth.

A little gasp sounded. "So hot. God, your mouth."

He hummed in response. Hell yes.

Flynn's legs closed around him again, then spread, then came back to cradle him, the movements restless.

This was fun. Blaine pulled steadily, humming around Flynn's prick. Flynn started babbling, calling him baby and telling him how good it was—how good *he* was. And it was all the truth—it was good. It was really good. Flynn tasted so right between Blaine's lips.

He felt really good, doing this, hanging out with Flynn, the heaviness that had been hanging over him gone. This was how he was supposed to feel when he was blowing his lover.

Blaine licked a little line around the ridge of Flynn's tip, teasing it, playing. Flynn's gasp was gratifying, as was the long, drawn-out moan that followed. Blaine smiled around the pretty cock, bobbing his head.

"So good. So hot and wet. Damn, you're amazing around my cock. Stunning. So good." The words kept flowing from Flynn like a babbling brook, and Blaine liked it. A lot.

Flynn's voice got higher pitched, the words losing any sort of sense, and that told Blaine it wasn't going to be long before his mouth was flooded with come. He reached down and rolled Flynn's balls.

"Blaine!"

The cry was heartfelt and sweet, followed by a rush of come into Blaine's mouth. He sucked and swallowed, sliding his tongue over the throbbing shaft.

Flynn dribbled a little more into his mouth as he shivered through a couple of aftershocks, and then he went limp, resting back against the couch. "Damn. Was good."

Blaine kissed the curve of Flynn's belly. "Your head okay?"

"Yeah, it only hurts when I laugh. Just kidding! It's fine." Flynn dragged a lazy hand through his hair.

"I'm so sorry, honey. I swear... it wasn't me."

"You don't have to keep apologizing, babe. I know it wasn't you. I know you had Christian's specter... on you? In you?" Flynn shivered. "If you keep apologizing, I'm going to start to think you really did do something wrong, and I'll beat you over the head about it."

"No more beating." Blaine wasn't that way.

"No, we've both been through enough. I just mean stop trying to convince me you did something you need to apologize for, because you didn't." Flynn sighed softly, his eyes drifting shut. "I could totally nap now that I've had a blow job of joy."

"Me too, love. Come on. I'll clean up later."

"We could nap right here on the sofa," Flynn suggested, looking for all the world like he was already asleep. He patted the cushion next to him.

"Brilliant, man." Blaine climbed up and half reclined at an angle to keep his hurt shoulder out of contact with the back of the couch.

Flynn snuggled right into his good side, and he fit. Perfectly. Like this was exactly where he was supposed to be. It was a little bit like magic.

Maybe it was all meant to be.

Chapter Seventeen

FLYNN couldn't believe they were back at the hospital. And that it had been his idea. He knew they needed it, though; they needed some closure. Besides, he was pretty sure the danger was gone. They'd uncovered what had really happened and dealt with the murderer. Christian's and David's ghosts could rest.

He just needed to go and see room 204 for himself and be sure.

Hell, with all the trouble, he'd never even been in here. How was that possible?

It was amazing how quickly it got dark once they were in the hospital. And Flynn had to work not to get spooked. They headed upstairs and crept along the hallway, all five of them sticking close together.

"Are you sure this is a good idea, Blaine?" Will whispered, and Blaine shook his head.

"Flynn needs to do it. Psycho." The smile Flynn got was warm, though, and Blaine didn't look worried.

"Yeah, yeah. We all need it—not just me. This needs to be closed for us. Besides, I bet you we can edit a hell of a show together out of what we've got, except we don't have a way to end it. This gives us one."

"I'm going to send it to a producer in Toronto," Jase said. "He wants to see it. He likes the blog."

Flynn looked over at Jase in surprise. "Seriously? That's so cool! We should have a party when we're done here."

"I'm all over that. We'll have a wrap party."

He smiled at Blaine. "We can host it at the barn."

Then he turned his attention back to room 204. The good news about the producer wanting to see their stuff and the party had him feeling far less freaked out by their environs, and he pushed the door open without any trepidation.

It looked the same—empty and bare and dusty. Old.

He looked around, half expecting to hear that voice screaming room 204. There was nothing, though. No voice, no cold spots, no specters or unexpected movements.

It was almost anticlimactic.

"Should we do some EVPs or something?" Jase asked.

"Can you guys not see that?" Blaine sounded shocked.

"What? Tell us what you're seeing, Blaine." Flynn looked around wildly, trying to spot what Blaine was witnessing.

"It's right there." Blaine grinned. "I hope we made it better. We tried."

"So I take it you're seeing Christian or David, or both of them?"

Come on, Blaine. Talk for the camera.

"It's just a shape. A fuzz."

"But you think it's someone in particular?" Flynn pushed.

Blaine shrugged. "Do you want to talk to someone?"

Flynn gasped as he suddenly felt something. He couldn't even describe what it was. Passing through cobwebs was the best he could do.

"Flynn? Flynn! It's on you."

He sidestepped and moved over toward Blaine, trying to get away from it.

Blaine grabbed his hand and tugged. "What do you want? Flynn's mine, you know. My lover."

"He knows." Flynn blinked, but the words that had come out of his mouth were true. He didn't know how he knew it, but he did. "I feel gratitude. He's grateful." Okay, this was freaking him out.

"Good. Good. Grateful is way better than vengeful."

"I think he wants us to have a long life together." Okay, it was still freaky as fuck, but at least the spirit didn't want to harm them. Blaine was right; this was way better than it had been.

"Well, if you want to say something, I've got the recorder right here. You can speak right into it."

Flynn snapped his mouth closed. He wasn't talking for this thing anymore. It was going to have to speak on its own.

"Just let yourself talk. It's okay. Christian told us. We know you were murdered, man. He told us."

Flynn's mouth opened without his volition, and a voice came out. A voice that wasn't his. "You got him. Thank you." Flynn stood there, his eyes huge. It was like someone had taken him over so he couldn't get his own words out, just these that didn't belong to him.

"You're welcome. Now. Please. Out of my Flynn, because that's creepy."

"Don't let it happen to you. You represent us."

Flynn suddenly felt like himself again, and he gasped, almost falling. "Oh my God. I never want to go through that again!"

"Can we fucking go? Now?" Darnell was gray, which was quite a feat, as dark-skinned as he was.

Flynn put a finger in the air and circled it. "Wrap it up first, because we are not coming back here. Ever. Just say something to wrap us up." He wanted out of here in the worst way possible and was trying to decide whether running out as soon as Blaine was done would be unmanly.

"That was probably the scariest thing we've experienced in days, and now we need to go back to the office and see what, if anything, we've recovered."

"Say something witty about the haunting of the hospital. Because I swear to God, I don't care what wrap-up shot anyone says we need to come back and tape, I'm not doing it. So we'd better have our bases covered." Flynn was done with this place and its body-jacking specters.

Blaine grinned with a glint in his eyes, looking tickled. "We've experienced all sorts of things here—from possession to spectral lights to voices. Hopefully we've helped lay all these ghosts to rest. I guess you could say we were going for a spiritual healing."

That actually made Flynn want to laugh, and he bit his lower lip to avoid it. Wouldn't do to appear glib and joking if they used that for the end of the potential show.

They all waited a few minutes. Then Will cackled. "A spiritual healing. That's what we should call it. 'The Haunting of the Eugene Thurston Memorial Hospital: A Spiritual Healing.'"

"Works for me," Darnell said. "Now can we get the fuck out of here and go home? I've had enough of hospitals for a lifetime."

"Amen to that," Flynn agreed.

The others all said something similar, and they headed out together, eager to have the Eugene Thurston Memorial Hospital behind them.

Chapter Eighteen

BLAINE waved as Jason pulled up with Flynn in the passenger seat. Flynn was enjoying his part-time job at Jason's company, running numbers and doing statistics for upper management. Blaine thought it sounded like hell, but money was money, and they didn't need help at the farm stand from Halloween through the spring.

Harvest goofiness was in full swing at the farm—a huge corn maze out back while apple cider, pumpkins, and tons of different local candies filled the little store. Soon they'd have to switch to Christmas and even shorter hours, and Blaine'd be in the barns with Dad more often than not, shoring things up and doing maintenance on the tractors.

It was weird how life went on outside of ghosts.

They'd taken everything they had (and didn't have) on the Eugene Thurston Memorial Hospital and turned it into a forty-minute video, using the story of Christian and David as the show's anchor, and sent it to Jason's producer friend/acquaintance. Now they were in wait-and-see mode.

Flynn popped out of the car and came over to give Blaine a quick, easy kiss. "Hey, babe."

"Hey, love. How was work?" He waved to Jason. "You coming in?"

"Can't! Have a meeting. I'll call later."

Flynn waved Jason off, and they watched as he turned the car around and headed back toward the city.

"Work was great. How about here?" Flynn asked as they headed inside.

"Been slow, but that's par for the course. The weather's beautiful, and tomorrow it'll be busy with the corn maze and all. Apple cider?"

"Yes, please. Especially if there's apple fritters or something to have with it. And I'm not working tomorrow. Can I help with the corn maze? It sounds like fun." Flynn ran his hand through his hair, the loose curls needing a cut.

"There's some muffins left. The fritters go fast, but we'll have some in the morning, and yes, please. That would be amazing—the extra hand and the company."

"Cool." Flynn stopped him before he got to the kitchen, turning him so they could kiss. It was nice and easy, almost lazy. There was a promise of passion in it, though, need that had been banked all day long.

They had discovered that their lives meshed easily. Even Mom and Dad adored Flynn. Hell, they loved having tech support on call.

It was good that the passion had continued even when the spectral weirdnesses had disappeared. Their connection hadn't been only because of the ghosts or the fact that both their birthdays had been the same day Christian and David died. Thank God. That would have totally sucked.

"You're thinking hard, honey," Flynn murmured, and Blaine flushed, cheeks going hot.

One of Flynn's eyebrows went up. "Now I'm really curious."

"Just thinking about how good it is. You and me, I mean."

"Oh." Flynn grinned and wrapped his arms around Blaine's waist, rubbing their middles together. "Yeah, it is, isn't it?"

"Yeah. Totally. I worried, you know, about the whole ghost thing."

"You were worried that's the only reason I was into you?" Flynn asked, hands sliding down to cup Blaine's ass and pull his groin in tighter against Flynn's.

"A little at first." Oh. Oh, that felt nice.

Flynn kissed him again, tongue lingering in his mouth before he pulled back. "And now?"

"Now I don't care why we got together. I love you."

"Oh, that was the right answer." Flynn kissed him again, harder this time. Then he rested their foreheads together.

"You wanna go home so I can show you just how much I love you too?"

"Help me close up and we can get there faster."

"Just tell me what veggies and fruit I can toss around and I'll be double-time quick."

"Mostly it's just putting the cider away and closing up."

"I know how to put the cider away." Flynn got to work, and if Blaine wasn't mistaken, there was a little extra wiggle to his walk.

"Can you pour us both some to take home?" He closed the windows and gathered the deposit.

"Sure." Flynn grabbed a couple of large mason jars and filled them with cider before continuing to put things away.

Together they managed, no sweat, and soon they were riding the four-wheeler up toward the farm. Flynn was snugged up behind Blaine, cock pressing hard against his ass as Flynn held on tight, arms wrapped around him.

"You're having a good day, love!"

Flynn's bright laughter carried to him, and Flynn squeezed him tighter. "I am now."

So amazing—the crisp, cool air, the scent of the apples and cider on the air, the pressure of Flynn behind him. Blaine almost did a lap around the farm to keep on enjoying it, but he wanted to get home even more, the promise in Flynn's hard cock too inviting to resist.

They parked the four-wheeler in the garage, then headed inside, arm in arm, Flynn carrying the basket with the jars of cider in it. Flynn set it down on the coffee table and waggled his eyebrows. "Come upstairs. I want you like whoa."

"I'm totally into whoa, Flynn."

Flynn laughed again, grabbed his hand, and tugged him upstairs. "Man, I laugh more with you than I ever have in my life."

"That's a good thing, isn't it?" Blaine figured it had to be. "You, me, the guys—it's all good."

"It's amazing." Flynn kissed him once they'd made it to the top of the stairs. "But I've got to tell you, I'm not talking about the guys right now. Just you and me."

"Just you and me, huh? I like that, being us."

"I do too." Flynn grabbed his shirt and tugged him into the bedroom. Then Flynn took Blaine's shirt off him, hands sliding on his chest. "I like it a lot."

"I like you." Blaine worked Flynn's belt open, popped his fly.

Flynn laughed once more, trying to suck in his belly at the same time, which totally didn't work and started him laughing even harder. "Me too. You, I mean. I like."

"You and me likey-likey," Blaine teased, then cracked up.

"Good thing we don't need to talk to make love," Flynn noted when he'd finally stopped cackling. He tugged at Blaine's jeans, doing a better job of getting them undone and off than Blaine had done with Flynn's. "Or we'd be in trouble."

"We managed to do this possessed and hurt and...." Blaine moaned as his fingers brushed the tip of Flynn's cock.

Flynn gasped softly, bucking toward him. "No talk of the other guys. No ghosts or possession talk either. Not when you've got your hand on my cock."

"I love how you feel in my hand. Have I said?" He stroked, base to tip.

"N-no, I can't say as you h-have." Flynn whimpered softly.

"I love touching you, getting you off."

"I love it when you do that too."

He kept rubbing, petting Flynn, making his lover need.

"Babe...," Flynn groaned and pushed closer to him. "Don't stop, 'kay?"

"I promise. I promise you. I won't stop."

"Good." Flynn hauled him in for another kiss, hands curling against Blaine's skin. The kisses made Blaine's eyes roll, made his balls draw up until they ached.

Flynn grabbed hold of his ass, and Blaine swore he could feel each digit as they squeezed him.

He moaned into their kiss, his fingers dragging over Flynn's delicate skin. Flynn's fingers tightened, and Blaine pushed into another delicious kiss. Flynn began to hump up into his touch, drive into his closed fist.

Panting moans filled his mouth, Flynn riding his hand faster, liquid heat easing the way. Flynn's fingers dug into his ass, tighter and tighter as he worked Flynn's cock.

"Tell me you'll make love to me, Flynn."

"Uh-huh. Yes. Gonna do it." Flynn pulled him closer, panting hard.

"Good." Okay, he was having a ball. "I want it. I want you, good and hard."

Flynn whimpered, cock getting even more rigid in Blaine's hand. He swooped down and wrapped his lips around Flynn's cockhead.

"Blaine!" Flynn shouted it loudly.

Yeah. Yeah, he felt like a stud.

Flynn sawed his hips, gently pushing his cock deeper into Blaine's mouth, and Blaine opened up, taking more, taking inch after inch. Flynn's noises got louder and louder as his orgasm got close. Blaine grabbed Flynn's hips and dragged them tighter together.

Blaine regretted it for a second, but only for a second, when Flynn cried out again and spunk poured down Blaine's throat, hot and salty. Flynn would get it back up—if not now, then after supper.

He kept sucking, cleaning Flynn gently as his lover panted, petting Blaine's head clumsily.

Blaine let his eyes close, let himself just float, head bobbing.

"Oh God. Keeping me hard."

That was sort of the point, wasn't it?

"Come on, babe. Bed. I want you."

He let Flynn's cock slip from his lips, kissing its tip on the way out. Flynn whimpered for him, a shiver working its way through the lovely body.

"Pretty man." Blaine knew he was being goofy, but he was a dude in love, and he felt like a million bucks.

"Not as pretty as you." Flynn stroked his cheek, then took a step backward. "Come on. We need to get horizontal."

"Uh-huh."

He stood there watching Flynn, who pulled the covers back and crooked his finger.

"Mmm." Flynn grabbed hold of him and tugged him down onto the bed so he was covering Flynn's warm body. Blaine tumbled hard, getting the wind knocked out of him.

Flynn wrapped around him, laughing as they kissed again. Blaine's cock bumped against Flynn's belly, nudging the warm skin. Flynn's laughter faded into a moan, his strong body bucking beneath Blaine.

"Touch me. Fuck me, huh? Please?"

"Yes." Flynn reached for the lube off the side table, running his free hand along Blaine's spine. He spread, straddling Flynn's thighs.

Humming, Flynn moved his fingers along Blaine's crack to tease the wrinkled little hole. They were hot, the touch just right.

"Want me to ride you?" Blaine asked, taking a kiss between each word.

"Oh…." Flynn's eyes crossed. "Yes. Yes, I do."

"'Kay. Get me ready for you."

"Yeah." Flynn splurted lube onto his fingers, then reached around Blaine again, fingers slick this time as they ran along his crack and then his hole. Blaine leaned down, ass up in the air, wiggling a little.

"Eager bunny," Flynn murmured, still sliding his fingers back and forth.

"I want you. It's like an ache."

"Let me kiss it better." Flynn pushed a finger into him, breaching his body.

"Oh…." He arched and took it, hips rolling.

Flynn groaned and pushed his finger deeper. God, Flynn made him a little dizzy, made him more than a little breathless.

Flynn fucked him for a few moments with just the one finger; then he pushed a second finger in with it.

"Mm. More, lover. Don't stop."

"I won't." Flynn pressed his fingers deep, and they glanced off Blaine's gland, lighting him up from the inside.

He climbed the headboard, driving himself down onto Flynn's fingers over and over. At some point, Flynn added another finger, working him with three, stretching him good and wide.

Blaine's eyelids fluttered, his heart hiccupping. Good. Good. God.

Flynn yanked his fingers away. "I need to be in you now, babe. Please. Get me a condom."

"Uh-huh." He leaned over and snagged one, tore off the cover, and rolled it over Flynn's cock.

Flynn opened and closed his hands, panting harshly. Blaine loved this—the way Flynn responded and wanted him.

"Come on, babe. Straddle my legs and take me in." Flynn reached for him and made grabby hands.

"Uh-huh." Blaine knelt up and then rubbed the tip of Flynn's cock against his hole, teasing them both.

Flynn's immediate groan made him feel a hundred feet tall. He bore down, taking Flynn in deep, one inch at a time.

"Blaine. Oh damn. So tight. Love it when you ride me."

It was all he could do to nod, moan, and agree. The pressure inside him was too big for anything else.

Flynn found his asscheeks again, fingers digging in and beginning to drive him up and down. They moved together, sweat popping up on Flynn's skin, making it shine. Blaine braced himself on Flynn's chest, his rhythm strong and steady as he bounced on Flynn's cock.

Flynn watched him, gaze running over his whole body, eyes alight.

"H-hey. Hey. Harder."

Flynn's knees came up behind him, and he knew Flynn was digging his heels into the mattress. A moment later, Flynn fucked up into him, hard.

"Jesus!" He sat up, rocking fast, his cock dripping on Flynn's belly.

Like those drops called to Flynn, he wrapped a hand around Blaine's cock. Every time Flynn thrust, it sent Blaine's cock through the tunnel of his hand. Blaine's toes curled hard, his entire body responding to the touch.

"So hot, babe." Flynn squeezed Blaine's cock tighter and began to drag his hand along its smooth length.

"Uhn." That had to count as a response, right? It was all Blaine had.

Flynn brought him down for another kiss, changing the angle of Flynn's cock inside him. Not deep enough, but a different sensation, which was welcome. He tightened his internal muscles around Flynn's prick, working it madly for a second.

"Fuck! Oh God!" Flynn jacked him base to tip, working him hard and making him gasp, drawing his need up to the very edge.

"Come on, come on," muttered Flynn, hips pushing up hard and fast, each word accompanied by a panting gasp.

"Come...." Blaine was going to. He was so close.

"Uh-huh." Flynn got a good pump in, the tip of his cock banging up against Blaine's gland pretty hard, sending lightning shooting through him, and he spurted, spraying heat over Flynn's hard belly.

Blaine's ass squeezed down on Flynn's cock again, making his lover cry out and buck a few more times. Then he leaned forward, resting on Flynn's chest.

Flynn ran his fingers along Blaine's spine again, all the way down to where they were still connected.

"Oh." He blinked slowly and squeezed Flynn's cock.

Flynn shivered, then sighed. "I should come out. I love how you feel around me, though."

"Love you too."

Flynn smiled and nodded. "Yes. Love *you*." With another soft sigh, Flynn pulled out, and Blaine shifted off him so he could deal with the condom. Then they settled together close.

"You think we could talk about going exclusive, Flynn? Barebacking, maybe?"

"Oh wow. I've never done that with anyone. As for exclusive—you're the only one for me, babe. I mean, forever."

"Forever, huh? You... you mean it?" Blaine had never thought in terms of always, not about anything.

"I do. I can feel it every time I look at you. Or think about you. Or talk to you."

Blaine didn't have the right words, so he just held on, squeezing Flynn tight. Flynn moaned for him, nuzzling.

Then the doorbell rang, and Flynn groaned.

"No way...." They were very busy being naked.

The banging started next. "I know you're in there, guys! Come on and let me in before I break down the door," Jason shouted.

"Hold on to your nuts!" Blaine called back. "Just a second!"

"Damn. I thought he had something to do?" Flynn grumbled, then took a kiss, pressing their mouths together and going for it.

Jason could wait a second more.

Their lips parted slowly, and Flynn smiled at him "Love you, Blaine."

"I love you. Like permanent, forever, long-term-partner kind of love."

Flynn's smile grew brilliant.

"Guys!" The banging started again.

"Jesus Christ! I'm coming!" Asshole.

Blaine grabbed his pants and tugged them on, stumbling shirtless down the stairs.

He hadn't reached the door yet when Flynn caught up with him and tossed him a T-shirt. "Can't have anyone ogling my man."

"Thanks, babe."

"You two quit canoodling!"

"Canoodling?" Flynn cracked right up.

"I swear to God I'm going to kick this door down."

That only made Flynn laugh harder.

"What's with the standing out here banging on the door?" Will's voice chimed in.

What the heck was going on?

"They won't let me in!"

A stronger pounding started. "Let us in."

Now it was Jase who was cackling. "Let us in by our chinnie-chin-chins."

Darnell's voice finished it. "Or we'll huff and we'll puff and blow your house down."

"Christ. You guys better have brought pizza!" Blaine unlocked the door.

All three of them tumbled in, Jase with a bag, Will with a two-four, and Darnell with three boxes of pizza. Oh good.

Flynn led the way to the living room. "I thought you were busy tonight, Jase?"

Jason shook his head. "I mean, yes, I was, but I'm done with that meeting, and that's why I wanted everyone here."

"Yeah, he wouldn't tell us a thing," Darnell noted. "Kept saying when we got here. Well, now we're all here, man. What's up?"

"Sit. Everyone. Sit."

They all sat, grumbling and elbowing each other as all four of them crammed themselves onto the couch facing Jason.

Jase regarded them, smiling. But he didn't say anything.

"Don't make me hurt you," growled Will.

Chuckling, Jase opened the bag he had carried in and pulled out a bottle of champagne. "You guys have glasses?"

"Tell us, already," Flynn insisted. "You interrupted a great moment, and I want to know why."

"I was speaking to Bob Cheering, the television producer I told you about."

"The one you sent the Eugene Thurston Memorial Hospital tape to," Flynn specified.

"That's the one."

"And?"

Jase just grinned and popped the cork on the champagne.

Blaine looked at his best friend, his heart crawling up in his throat. "No shit, man? They picked us up?"

Jase nodded, laughing as Flynn fist pumped the air and Will jumped up to grab Jase around the waist and lift him right off the ground, almost spilling the champagne. Darnell whooped, the sound incredibly loud.

"Oh my God. Oh my God. Guys! We did it!" Blaine leaned over to Flynn and kissed him hard. "We did it!"

Flynn grabbed his head and kissed him back. Long and hard. Long enough the guys started catcalling and shouting out "Get a room."

Laughing, Flynn let him go. "We did it."

"We did."

"Glasses," Jase said. "Come on, Blaine, man. Glasses."

Flynn goosed him as he got up, all happy smiles and a wicked twinkle in his eyes.

Blaine hurried to the kitchen and grabbed five glasses. They weren't champagne flutes, but it didn't matter. They didn't have champagne lives.

The guys were all laughing and cheering when he got back, the air electric with excitement.

He held the glasses, Jase poured, and then they all stood and held up their drinks.

"We did it." Will was all grins.

Darnell just hooted again, holding his glass high.

"Way to go, everyone," Flynn said, looking them each in the eye.

"To us! To the Supernatural Explorers! Five gay ghost hunters!"

They all clinked glasses and drank the champagne down. Flynn looked over at Blaine, a light shining in his eyes.

They'd done it. It had taken all of them, but they'd done it.

"So what exactly does this mean?" Flynn asked.

"It means they want a dozen more shows. It means enough money to make those shows. It means we're going to premiere in June for the summer season."

Blaine sat, still holding Flynn's hand. He needed to tell his folks.

"Oh my God! That's amazing. A dozen shows? With the money up front to make them? That's amazing," Flynn said again.

"We'll have to be frugal, but yeah. Yeah. All we have to do is make our shows." Jason looked over, eyes twinkling. "And if you could arrange another possession, Blaine, that would totally rock."

"No way!" Flynn shook his head. "Not happening. Not even pretend."

"Are you sure, man? They loved that in the previews…."

"You all willing to take your turns?" Flynn asked.

Oh, nice one. Blaine snorted, knowing full well that the guys considered him the front man.

"Right. He's the face of the outfit. They love your look, by the way. Love your story." Jase nodded, grinning like a fool. "They want us to focus on LGBT stories, spirits."

"Rock on. That's great. It means we'll get to be ourselves. And of course they love Blaine's look. What's not to love?" Flynn touched his cheek, eyes warm.

"God help us and save us from newlyweds." Darnell poured himself a second glass of champagne and drained it. "Ahh. Now let's eat."

"I hope you got all our favorites," Flynn said, beginning to open the various pizza boxes. "Oh, green olive and sausage. You rock."

They all settled with their slices and their beers—
champagne was all well and good, but pizza needed beer.
Flynn leaned against Blaine, right where he belonged.

They were doing it. Them. All together.

Blaine looked up and saw a woman standing
behind Flynn, smiling, her eyes the same as her son's.

Yeah. Yeah, okay. They were totally doing this.

Coming in November 2017

DREAMSPUN BEYOND

Dreamspun Beyond #7
Camp H.O.W.L. by Bru Baker

Moonmates exist, but getting together is going to be a beast.

When Adrian skipped his "werewolf puberty," he assumed he was—somehow—human. But he was wrong, and he's about to go through his Turn with a country between him and his pack, scared, alone—and eight years too late.

Dr. Tate Lewis's werewolf supremacist father made his Turn miserable, and now Tate works for Camp H.O.W.L to ease the transition for young werewolves. He isn't expecting to offer guidance to a grown man—or find his moonmate in Adrian. Tate doesn't even believe in the legendary bond; after all, his polygamist father claimed five. But it's clear Adrian needs him, and if Tate can let his guard down, he might discover he needs Adrian too.

A moonmate is a wolf's missing piece, and Tate is missing a lot of pieces. But Adrian is up to the challenge.

Dreamspun Beyond #8
Ante Up by Kim Fielding

Love is a high-stakes game.

A century and a half ago, Ante Novak died on a Croatian battlefield—and rose three days later as a vampire. Now he haunts Las Vegas, stealing blood and money from drunken gamblers and staying on the fringe of the powerful vampire organization known as the Shadows. His existence feels empty and meaningless until he meets beautiful Peter Gherardi, who can influence others with his thoughts.

An attraction flares instantly, bringing life to Ante's dead heart. But the Shadows want Peter too, and they're willing to kill to get him. As Ante and Peter flee, they learn more about themselves and each other, and they discover that the world is a stranger place than either of them imagined. With enemies at their heels and old mistakes coming back to exact a price, can Ante and Peter find sanctuary?

CPSIA information can be obtained
at www.ICGtesting.com
Printed in the USA
FFOW03n0932260418
46366957-48067FF